six days in September

JEFFREY GRISAMORE

Six Days in September

Cover and interior design by Asya Blue
Cover illustration and title lettering by Alexandria Manson

Published in the United States

ISBN 978-1-7368905-1-6 (paperback)
ISBN 978-1-7368905-0-9 (hardcover)
ISBN 978-1-7368905-3-1 (e-book)

I would have loved you even if we'd never met.

"No matter how much time passes, no matter what takes place in the interim, there are some things we can never assign to oblivion, memories we can never rub away."

— Haruki Murakami

FOREWORD

My grandfather was a Methodist minister in Iowa. A circuit rider going from church-to-church on Sunday mornings in the early 1900s on a motorcycle. When I was a young boy he told me the story of his calling – that's what they call it when God touches you and asks you into his service. He said when he was seven years old, he burst into the house with tears streaming down his face one summer day after playing outside in the yard on the family farm in rural southwestern Iowa, and when his mother asked him what was wrong, he said, "I don't want to be a minister." His mother told him he didn't have to, but from that day forward, he was singular in his mission to preach the gospel, which he did until he died some 90 years later.

My story in Alaska, those six days in September, is similar in form and function. I was also touched by God but in a very different way. I fell in love with a woman in Alaska during a fishing trip. The only way I can explain it is to say that I believe a power greater than myself interceded in my life and showed me the great white light of love. A woman much younger than me grabbed my heart and made me hers for a very short time. I would like to think I made her mine too, but I'm not sure. She showed me what it can be about and by 'it' I mean true love and pure life. Angels can save you just by their touch or their presence and I think that's what happened to me.

Love is not what I thought it would be. It's something greater, more powerful and elusive and in my case more fleeting, but still something surely sent by God.

CHAPTER ONE

"In the depth of winter, I finally learned that there was in me an invincible summer."

—Albert Camus

In the half-light of the early Alaskan evening, the Cessna 185 Skywagon touched down on the dirt landing strip and the engine coughed and sputtered to idle speed as the plane lurched to a parking spot close to the end of the crude landing strip. The sky was clear, the temperature was warm, the landing strip was soft and forgiving, and the air was ripe with the thick aroma of late summer in the bush. Pure wildness. Black cottonwoods, aspen, and Sitka spruce grew erratically over the landscape like soaring apostles, their fragrance carpeting the airfield in an aromatic fog as their leaves waved in the light breeze.

I released my seat belt, took off my headphones, opened the plane's passenger door, and stepped down onto the soft dirt. My backpack and fly rod were stowed behind the front seat, which I slid forward and grabbed the gear. I got out, slammed the dented metal door closed behind me, turned the latch, and gave a thumbs-up to the pilot. He turned the plane and taxied back down the runway, turned again to position himself, then gunned the engine, roared down the runway toward me and lifted off just before he reached me standing at the end of the runway. The airstrip was located a hundred yards from the lodge at the top of a steep hill, in a spot where the terrain leveled off to a plateau of sorts. The plane reemerged over the tops of the tall spruce that surrounded the lodge and headed back to Anchorage, its red strobe light flickering as it disappeared into the early evening sky, the drone of its engine gradually fading into the milieu of the wilderness soundscape.

I turned and walked to the end of the crude airstrip. A small group of people were waiting for me there: my friend and owner of the camp, Caleb Stout, the fishing guide Micah, Maddie the cook, and a young woman I didn't recognize who looked like she was about 25 years old. She had long, light brown hair, high cheekbones, and hazel eyes and was dressed in jeans and flip-flops and a western-style pearl snap-button shirt.

Caleb and I embraced, then I greeted Maddie and Micah. The woman I didn't know stepped forward and shook my hand. I noticed her hands were rough with calluses. There were small cuts on her fingers and palm and she had short, unpolished nails. Her handshake was strong, her fingers long and slim. She was tall and athletic and had exceedingly long straight hair, nearly down to her waist.

"Hi Eli, I'm India," she said. "I'm helping at the camp these days. You're staying in the cabin up here." She gestured toward the small cabin just a few yards from where we were standing. "Do you need help with your bag?" she asked, smiling.

She pulled back her hair, wrapped it into a ponytail and tied the ponytail into itself. Her jeans were low cut and her shirt was short around her midriff, showing a taut muscular stomach; her shirtsleeves were rolled up showing equally muscular arms. Both her jeans and tan western-style shirt were stained.

"Nice to meet you, India. And no, I'm fine, I've stayed in the cabin before so I'm good. Thanks," I said.

"Okay, come down to the lodge for a beer and dinner when you get unpacked," India said.

She turned and walked back down the hill toward the lodge with Caleb, Micah, and Maddie. I picked up my gear and walked the few yards to my cabin. I stowed my gear in the one dresser and used some hooks on the wall for my jackets, opened the two side windows that looked out over the runway as well as the front door and then went out to the cabin's small porch and sat in an old chair. Lucy, the yellow lab who was the camp mascot, ambled up the hill from the lodge for a visit. We spent a few minutes getting reacquainted, me stroking her head, both of us admiring the sweeping vista in front of us. The runway was the only level land as far as I could see. Low cascading hills intersected one another in every direction I looked. Where the hills met, I knew, there was almost always a small stream or waterfall. As far as the eye could see there was a never-ending quilt of unimaginable colors: fire engine reds, yellows, deep greens. Macaroon hills interrupted by licorice colored valleys with cobalt blue clumps of late-season blueberries so vibrant you could see them from a distance.

After a few minutes I rose from my chair and walked slowly down the path to the lodge with Lucy in tow, checking out the vast wilderness panorama as I walked. It was warm out, but there's always the slightest bit of coolness in the Alaskan air, especially this far north. The pale blue early-evening sky was just beginning to have a pink cast to it as a late afternoon haze rolled in off the mountains to the north. I reached the bottom of the trail, climbed the stairs to the lodge's deck, opened the side door and entered. The kitchen was just as I remembered it. Rustic and smelling of fresh-baked bread, the rich aroma mixed with the smell of balsam poplar burning in the fireplace in the great room which dominated the first floor. Maddie was at the stove. Caleb in the living room with Micah tying flies and talking about tomorrow. India stood by the sink peeling potatoes for dinner, her back turned toward the door. She looked over her shoulder when the door slammed behind me and gave me a wide smile. The ponytail she'd gathered her hair into when we were all standing by the airstrip was draped over the front of her shirt. She wiped her wet hands on her apron and moved across the room to me.

"Hi. Can I get you a beer?"

"No, thanks, I'll go. I need to stretch my legs. How about you?"

"No – but we're almost ready for dinner." She smiled and moved away.

I walked through the low-ceilinged, split-log kitchen out onto the deck that wrapped around the lodge. I went down a long set of outdoor stairs to the shop building where the provisions were stored behind locked steel casements that for the most part managed to keep the bears out. I found a glass and poured myself a beer through a tap on the refrigerator, then went out to the lawn between the lodge and the river, my boots sinking into the soft grass, Lucy by my side, and sat on a sawed-off tree stump that sat in the middle of the yard. This was one of my favorite places. You could stand here on the lawn just twenty yards from the river and watch as the sun began to set over the foothills of the Alaska Range. Tonight, the light was seemingly translucent in the dusty glow of an early September evening. I could see for miles. It was still early evening but the sun was warm on my face. The lush green grass smelled warm and rich. Lucy lay down beside me and groaned as she settled in against my leg.

In this part of Alaska all the lakes and streams result from glaciers that moved through the region over two million years ago, forming the Alaska Range. The gate-keeper of that range is Denali, which is Athabascan for *The Great One*, the largest peak in North America at 23,240 feet. The Aningan river, known locally as the Ann, cuts a wide ribbon through central Alaska, originating at Smith Lake, a nearly inaccessible lake up near the Alaska Range, then winds its way to the Cook Inlet near Anchorage after joining the Gold River. The Ann flows within 50 yards of the lodge, full and lazy there with long sweeping bends. This evening it held a particularly soft glow as it was kissed by the fading sunlight of the early evening. I could see a fine mist coming off the water.

Across the river, the foothills of the Alaska range, beginning their rise toward the north, looked like an undulating carpet stretching as far as the eye could see.

A noise distracted me, and I turned. India was coming out of the shop. She noticed Lucy and me, stopped, and leaned against the edge of the building giving me an inquisitive look, her head cocked and a dishrag held loosely in her hand. Her apron, now stained with some red spots, was still on.

"Beautiful, isn't it?" she said.

"I'm not sure I've ever seen such a completely clear evening sky in Alaska," I said, turning back and staring at the river.

"We had rain almost every day two weeks ago but then it cleared, and since then we've had an unending supply of beautiful weather that we haven't seen for some time. The streams should be perfect for fishing this week, or at least the first part of the week."

I kept watching the river, losing touch with the moment as I often do, the view in front of me taking me to some other place. I get distracted this way. People can be disruptive, nature can't. It wasn't as if I felt disrupted by India. But there was some obscure emotion rising in me, some profound attraction that I didn't quite know what to do with.

"Caleb tells me you're from New York."

"Yeah," I said. When I tell people I'm from New York it nearly always causes a pause and then much more conversation. But I didn't want to go through all that now. It felt too good to be here – I just wanted to look.

"Lucy likes you," she said as Lucy shifted closer to my right and leaned against my side.

"And I like her. She saved my life last year."

I told her about how the previous year, in the middle of the night, a mature male black bear chased Lucy around the deck a time or two and followed her into the house. Lucy's barking woke up Caleb and he ran down the stairs into the kitchen and shot the bear as it charged toward him. It was one of those stories that lasts a lifetime and gets longer and better as the years progress, even though when it happened we were terrified.

"I heard about that. You were here?" she asked.

"I was and I won't forget it, believe me. I was staying at the cabin next door and I heard Lucy barking, then Caleb yelling, then the gunshot. Some way to wake up. Lucy had run outside for a quick check of the deck and the next thing you know she was on a dead run, barking, screaming really, and a big black bear was on her tail, straight into the house and closing fast."

"We haven't had anywhere near the bear problems this year, although we still see them every day. But don't worry. If one shows up I'll protect you. Are you all set for tomorrow?"

"We're going together?" I asked.

"Yeah. We're going up Ann Creek. I just started as a guide here but I've been fishing my entire life. Things here are more relaxed this week because it's late in the season, so I'm guiding if that works for you. I can't wait to get on the water. But for now, let's go have dinner."

Dinner at the lodge was an intimate and relaxing affair. Maddie was a world-class camp cook who took the provisions Caleb provided plus whatever she could harvest in the garden and transformed the raw ingredients into powerfully good food. A wiry, tough outdoorswoman, Maddie was an accomplished chef with a touch that belied her quiet demeanor. On my previous trip she'd transformed the bear that invaded the lodge into the finest pate' imaginable, with the rest of the meat providing endless meals of bear lasagna.

Tonight we had honey-lemon-coated salmon that she cooked on a cedar plank in an outdoor oven Caleb had built on the deck, along with copious amounts of fresh vegetables grown in a still-abundant garden followed by plentiful dessert.

After dinner on most nights Caleb retired to the great room with guitar in hand and anybody who wasn't ready for bed joined him and we all sat around singing old folk songs, and tonight was no exception. Those songs made the soft rustic surroundings seem even more quaint and reflective.

The great room was the hub of activity in the lodge. It was paneled in knotty pine like the rest of the lodge. A huge bull-moose head was mounted over the fireplace that stood sentinel along the long back wall and a long dining room table sat on the other side of the room in front of a long picture window that looked out over the river and extended the length of the room. You could easily seat twenty people at the table. Two large sectional couches and a number of overstuffed recliners filled every square inch of the rest of the living room. The walls were adorned with all manner of game and fish, testimony to the storied history this place held for adventurous hunters and fisherman willing to travel to a place this remote.

Caleb's favorite song was the Johnny Horton classic *"North to Alaska."* He sang it as a slow, mournful tale—not the upbeat version made famous in the '50s. Listening to his version, one could envision generations of frontiersmen facing the realities of the harshest and potentially most rewarding land in the world. The words as he sang them had a haunting ring: *"George turned to Sam with my gold in my hand, said Sam you're a lookin' at a lonely man - I'd trade all the gold that's buried in this land for one small band of gold to place on sweet little Jenny's hand, cause a man needs a woman to love me all the time – remember Sam, a true love is hard to find…a-go North to Alaska, go North, the rush is on."*

As I sat in the great room listening to him I found myself transfixed by the song and by his singing. His songs were mostly slow stories of hardship, and I wondered if that reflected Caleb's time in Alaska too or just a musical preference. I suspected the former. Tonight the room was quiet as he sang, and everyone in the camp ventured in to lean on a table or sit by the roaring fire. He wasn't a master player, or even a good singer for that matter, but his songs had weight to them. They were worth listening too.

Afterwards I went outside to the deck and sat overlooking the area between the lodge and the river, watching as the dusk continued to yield to nightfall in the late summer sky. Micah came out and sat beside me tying flies and we caught up as the rest of the camp prepared for the night—the sound of plates being washed, pots clanging, and people saying good night the only noises coming from the house.

Eventually Micah went inside and after a few minutes India quietly appeared, now in stocking feet. She sat down on the chaise across from me, clicked the chaise back a few notches to get to a reclining position, breathed a deep sigh, and looked up into the night sky. I settled back more deeply into my chair and looked at what was left of the cloudless sky above us, a catching moon arriving from the east, the direction of home. The constellations were in full bloom and looking close - like you could reach up and touch them. My life in New York seemed distant now—the meetings, the clients, the commute, the intensity and immediacy of it all, the never-ending rush, seemed a million miles away. Living in New York is like being awake twenty-four hours a day and it was always easy for me to summon the anxiety of leaving my life there, but not tonight. Not here.

I looked over at India and saw that she had fallen asleep within minutes of lying back in the chaise. She had turned on her side and was curled into the fetal position. I watched her from across the deck: strands of loose hair coming out of her ponytail and falling onto her face, her jaw slightly ajar as she relaxed and fell deeper and deeper into sleep. Her waist-length ponytail spread out over her like a blanket as she lay on her side.

After thirty minutes or so and with the last of the light ebbing, I stood up to take my empty beer glass into the kitchen. The sound of my chair scraping on the deck as I got up woke her and she sat up and stretched, yawned, laughed quietly, deeply, and sheepishly, and said she was sorry for falling asleep. We sat for a moment in the almost darkness, the lush fragrance on the breeze wafting over us, enveloping us as in a warm blanket, the house now quiet behind us.

"Time for sleep. We have an early morning tomorrow," she said.

"I'll walk you to your cabin." I said.

I took her hand and helped her to her feet, and we walked down the deck stairs and over the grassy lawn. Saw-whet and boreal owls called and a pack of coyotes began barking in the distance. The coyotes sounded like a mixture of adults and year-ling pups, the latter crying more than barking as if they were trying to keep up with the others. The result was a wilderness hymn that I envisioned to be a celebration of the coyotes' freedom and remoteness. Mysterious and enchanting at the same time. Animals so wild and yet so close—no threat to us but a reminder that this little camp was essentially an island in the deep, dense wilderness.

We stopped at India's cabin and she went inside and walked across the room in near darkness to light an oil lamp beside the bed while I stood at the door holding a headlamp so she could see. The electricity for the whole camp was powered by a generator run on diesel fuel flown in from Anchorage each week, and to conserve electricity and diesel, the generator was shut off at ten-thirty every night and turned back on at six-thirty in the morning.

"I'll say goodnight and see you in the morning," I said. She turned and looked back at me, her eyes were aglow in the oil lamp light, which cast shadows across the room, her face backlit by the lamp. She slowly ran her hands through her long hair, loosening the kinks where it had been held in place by the rubber band. She looked different with her hair down, older, more mature. I wasn't sure what to make of her but there was something about her that was captivating. She seemed as wild and elusive as this wilderness. Not wild in a social sense, but wild as in free and unobtainable—evanescent.

She crossed the room, leaned against the edge of the door jamb next to me, and paused for a long moment, not looking at me but beyond me out onto the lawn, a serious look in her eyes. Then she looked back at me and smiled. "Goodnight," she half-whispered and closed the door. I turned and made the short walk up to the landing strip to my cabin.

In early September, the sun in Alaska sets around 9:30 p.m., which is better for sleeping than in July when I normally came. In early July just after the summer solstice, the sun doesn't technically set until just before midnight, and even then, is more dusk than dark. You can easily walk anywhere without need of a flashlight as late as 1:00/1:30 a.m., and for the most part you can see all night long.

During the ten or twelve times I had been to Alaska and stayed at Caleb's camp, I had been awakened almost nightly by the sound of the grizzlies who cut through the camp from the river and used the runway as a path to the forest. Hearing them grunting and snorting as they walked by my little cabin was a chilling reminder that they owned this property and you were only a guest at their pleasure. Although the .357 magnum that I kept tucked under my pillow provided only a small measure of protection, it was the only deterrent available if one of the bears decided to come into the cabin.

It was quarter of eleven when I got to my cabin. On this night I hit the lower bunkbed and was instantly asleep, the travels of the day providing a sleep-inducing haze that I couldn't resist.

CHAPTER TWO

"Days in whose light everything seems equally Divine, opening a thousand windows to show us God."

—John Muir

I was shocked from my sleep by a wet dog lick and the sound of a tail beating against the split-pine wall of my cabin. I opened my eyes and stared eyeball to eyeball with Lucy, who was impatient to get the morning started. Her head moving back and forth in reverse time to her tail wagging, her whole body in motion, as labs are prone to do. How she got into the cabin was unclear. I acceded to her demand for attention, swung a leg out, and sat up on the bed. After a moment I got up out of the lower bunk, stopped quickly in the bathroom to splash cold water on my face, and went out to the porch with Lucy, both of us basking in the bright sunshine of the early morning Alaska day. A light breeze was cascading down the landing strip, rustling the wild flowers and trees that surrounded the cabin. The smell of flowers and mountain tannin hung in the air. I looked across the valley that separated the camp from Chalktaw Mountain. Chalktaw is the largest mountain in the area but compared to the Alaska range it's just a large hill. The morning sunshine cast a filtered haze onto the view and I thought of my father, who taught me everything I knew about nature and the outdoors and gave me the same unquenchable thirst to participate in it that he had. I was sorry he had never had the opportunity to see this beautiful place. He would never have left.

With Lucy in tow, I turned and went back into the cabin to prepare for the day. I took a quick hot shower, brushed my teeth, ran my fingers through my short hair. I put on jeans and a t-shirt underneath a long-sleeved plaid shirt and grabbed my waders, baseball hat, and sunglasses. I also took my small fly bag and my rod. I tucked the .357 into my waist pack as I left the cabin and walked down to the lodge for breakfast.

Breakfast at the camp generally started at around 6:30, but today things didn't get going until 7:30. As I approached the lodge I saw India working at the sink through the kitchen window, the sun pouring onto her features, highlighting her, her face devoid of makeup. Unintentionally, I stopped and stood on the path and watched her for a long moment. She glanced up from the sink and caught me staring at her. She smiled broadly, brushed back the locks of hair that had fallen forward into her face with the back of her wet hand, and motioned me into the lodge kitchen with her head. When I entered the kitchen, she held out a cup of coffee and gave me a warm smile.

"Sleep well?" she asked.

"Very. Although I was rudely awakened by a crazy lab."

"She was sitting by your front door so I took the liberty of letting her in. I didn't think you'd mind—I had to go to the shed, so I let her say hello. You were sound asleep."

"Clearly."

Breakfast was the usual offering of eggs, bacon, pancakes, and plenty of coffee. After breakfast it was time to start fishing, and India and I met Caleb at the upper helicopter landing pad located just next to my cabin. We stowed our gear in the storage cases bolted to the side frame of the chopper, jumped in, and were soon airborne.

Caleb was an exceptional pilot and the scenery below was breathtaking. As we flew over a small pond we saw a bull moose standing in the middle of it shaking his massive rack, swaying back and forth in a rage at the noise of our chopper intruding on his otherwise quiet morning, as if he thought he could pluck our invading nuisance from the sky. We flew north toward the first valley off the Alaska range, where the water and the land were even more unspoiled, traveling in the general direction of Denali and several key fishing sections of upper Ann Creek. We saw a sow grizzly with her two cubs below as well as a lone black wolf and other animals. Every species we saw was on a journey, on the move.

India sat between Caleb and me. All three of us had headphones on and the conversation was animated and rapid fire – we pointed out everything that appeared beneath us – animated and laughing. After twenty minutes in the air Caleb found a small sandbar in the middle of the stream and set the chopper down amidst a blinding storm of rock and sand. We wouldn't see him again until 5:00 p.m.—eight hours from now, with no ability to communicate with him or anyone at camp. We would be completely cut off, on our own with no backup. That was part of the allure.

We hurriedly exited the chopper, heads down, grabbed our gear, and sat huddled together by the stream as the chopper lifted off, pelting us with sand and gravel as it became airborne. It banked sharply to avoid the alder bushes and spruce lining the stream and roared off, heading back to camp.

We stood side by side on the sandbar and watched the chopper disappear into the morning sky. I glanced over at the stream next to us, slashing its way south – it was running strong today and the sound of the rushing water was loud. India strapped a 12-gauge pistol grip shotgun across her shoulders, then hoisted the backpack onto her strong frame. I offered to carry the pack, but she insisted. Within five minutes of landing, we were walking up the stream toward the first section of fishable water. The upper Ann was a tightly coiled ribbon of the cleanest gin-clear water on the planet. A few salmon were still in the stream but most were close to death, having made the journey to their ancestral home and deposited their eggs and now, in complete exhaustion, they began to die. But there were plenty of rainbows.

This section of Ann Creek was punctuated at every bend with deep green pools that held them. We started fishing at around nine a.m., when the hatches started. Mayflies, caddis, stoneflies, midges, and dragonflies – all in abundance on a day with ripe sunshine and warm temperatures.

Each turn of the stream offered new stunning scenery. Log jams up to ten feet high littering the stream from previous floods, oxbow bends where pools could get twenty feet deep to almost always surprising a bear or an otter or a beaver or worst case, a moose, every turn was filled with expectation. The riverbank was imprinted with paw prints of everything that lived in the area – fox, marten, wolves, beaver, otter, moose, and most especially bear. The bear tracks were the size of dinner plates or bigger, and some just minutes old. The character of the stream was deceiving – sometimes it was narrow and fast and at other times wider and slow moving, but never more than twenty feet wide at any point.

Several times during the morning we saw the same set of fresh bear tracks – it looked like a sow grizzly and two cubs. About an hour into the day we caught a glimpse of her upstream. The sow looked annoyed at our presence but kept fishing with her cubs since we were a safe distance away. She was ahead of us maybe 200 yards. Every few minutes she looked up and twice she rose to her back feet—standing maybe eight feet tall—trying to smell us so she could identify who was following them. About an hour after we first saw her, we nearly walked up on her as we rounded a tight bend in the river and there she was, standing 50 yards away – too close to ignore or walk away from. We were trapped. She stared at us, showed us her teeth, and started bawling loudly, standing upright, rocking back and forth, and her head rolling from side to side, her mouth wide open and salivating and her teeth gnashing. She was clearly agitated. India quickly dropped the pack, moved the gun off her shoulder, and chambered a round as we backed up slightly. This got the bear more agitated and it suddenly dropped to all fours and lunged at us, the cubs behind her and off to the side. India fired a flash bang – a shot that explodes in mid-air, designed to scare away anything approaching with its thunderous explosion. The bear stopped her charge but continued to walk slowly toward us, growling and rolling her head from side to side. India shot another flash bang over the bears head. After a few moments of growling and staring at us, she turned and walked back upstream to her cubs, looking back at us every few seconds, still threatening but no longer an immediate problem.

"Holy shit," I said.

"Damn," India said, her face red. "Let's get out of here. Slowly back away a few steps and let her decide to leave, we want her to understand that we aren't a threat."

It took a good fifteen minutes of looking upstream, while walking backwards downstream as slowly as possible, to ensure that the bear had backed off and was well outside a threat area to us.

Finally, I looked over at India. She smiled and said calmly, "Welcome to Alaska."

17

We laughed, and the laughing was like the valve on a pressure cooker, letting the tension escape. We found a place to sit on the gravel bar while we reloaded the shotgun, adjusted our gear, and had some water, then we cautiously resumed fishing, staying in the same place so the bear could walk farther away from us.

After that the day got progressively warmer and calmer and we got back into the rhythm of casting flies and landing rainbows. India spoke first after a long silence. "You're the only person who comes here alone."

"I'm sure," I responded.

"Why?"

"I didn't have anyone to come with. I only have one friend who's a good enough fisherman and outdoorsman to want to do this, and he just came back from a family vacation to Australia and didn't want to be gone again. And sometimes it's nice to be alone on a trip like this and just relax and not have to worry about anyone else. I spend most of my time alone anyway."

At this point we were fishing side by side about 25 feet apart. She looked over at me but offered no response. Effortlessly, she cast her line across the narrow water, her sunglasses precluding my view of her eyes. She was at one with the rod, the water, the stream, and I felt like maybe I was an intrusion, an obligation to be fulfilled that disrupted the spirit of the moment for her. I also felt she was as unsure about me as I was about her.

We moved upstream together, mostly in silence, and continued to cast in the syncopated rhythm of two fishermen caught in the moment, deep within their individual thoughts yet always intensely focused on the water, the holes, the fish, the topography, the signs the river, which if you watch closely enough, will always lead you to making the right decisions.

Fishing has been described by everyone from Hemingway to MacLean, Irving to Thoreau, because of the mysticism it holds. It's hard to explain the place you can go mentally when you fish, the way you can't describe a dream no matter how hard you try. Enlightenment. Pure consciousness.

Herbert Hoover may have come closest to describing it: *"To go fishing is the chance to wash one's soul with the pure air, with the rush of the brook, or with the simmer of sun on blue water. It brings meekness and inspiration from the decency of nature…patience towards fish, a mockery of profits and egos, a quieting of hate, a rejoicing that you do not have to decide a thing until next week and it is discipline in the equality of men − for all men are equal before fish."*

We fished the stream in fan style − each of us casting upstream and drawing the fly back across the water in an arc that ended downstream of us—at the same time slowly walking upstream – just a few steps at a time – covering the water slowly but thoroughly, never hitting the same line twice. We used different flies, so the same pattern wasn't presented to the same fish twice, with the upstream fisherman – India in this case – fishing salmon eggs while I fished a dry fly. Fish in Alaska are hungry and smart, seldom hitting the same fly a second time but certainly less particular than trout in the Lower 48. There are simply not enough months of open water for them to be overly choosy. They need to eat a year's supply of food in three months. If instead of salmon eggs there's a shrew or midge or nymph floating on or near the surface, they will hit hard and fast as long as the presentation is perfect. That, the presentation, is the fisherman's job, and the better the presentation the better the chances of a strike.

India was perfection on the water. In the flat morning sunshine I watched as she repeatedly lifted her line off the water, droplets shining in the sun as they were shed from her line when she brought it behind her where she hesitated a split second, then cast the line upstream, the line unfurling slowly, the fly dropping silently and without a splash onto the water, most of the time resulting in a strike or at least a rise. Her cast was like a metronome, it had a consistent cadence and rhythm. She didn't muscle the line or rod, but rather allowed it to do it's job and the result were inspiring.

As we walked upstream the morning sun gave way to early midday and the only sound that broke our silence was a small squeal of delight as one or the other of us pulled a three-pound rainbow trout out of the stream that at this point was deceptively small, no more than ten to twelve feet wide.

"So, you were raised here?" I asked.

"Yeah. My mother was originally from Illinois and my father was from Ohio. They came to Alaska in the late 1970s and decided to move into the bush and homestead. My brother and sister and I were all born at home and raised in the bush, completely removed from modern society other than the occasional trip to Anchorage. We didn't have electricity when I was young—no grocery stores, no television, no phone, no reliable well, home schooling—just family and a survival subsistence."

"Crazy," I said.

"I guess. I haven't lived any other way so I don't know the difference, but I know it hasn't been easy for my parents. They worked hard to provide for us in a very hostile and unforgiving environment. We didn't have anything other than oil lamps and a fireplace for most of my childhood and that comes with a certain hardship."

"Why'd they come here?"

"I really don't know. Just a desire to write their own chapter, I guess – it was the 70's and a time of freedom. My sense is that my dad drove the decision – Alaska was his siren song, I think. The adage is that people in Alaska are either running to or running from something, and that's probably true of him. I think he was running away from himself and to a place where there are hardly any rules.

"He's an extremely difficult man who doesn't fit into traditional society. Highly confrontational, as if someone is always out to get him or us. He's overtly conservative, and by that I mean far right. His first instinct is to think someone, or something is trying to screw him. Alaska was and is the perfect place for him. He can do what he wants and be left alone to his own devices, not dependent on anyone or anything. His personality and opinions would draw attention down in the Lower 48, but they're run of the mill in Alaska. There's lots of people like him up here. And there's something else." India hesitated as if weighing whether to mention the next part. She swallowed and looked at me.

"Over the last few years he's developed a nasty alcohol habit that appears to be getting worse. It started with a drink before dinner and it morphed into many drinks before and after dinner. It makes him more unpredictable and unbalanced, and he's getting more volatile. Combine that with his normal distrust of everyone, his hair trigger temper, two tours in Vietnam, and you've got a recipe for awful things happening.

"It's been especially hard on my mother. She's old beyond her years. I think she may move into Anchorage soon - I have an aunt who is requiring more care, and I think Mom is looking forward to the opportunity to have a different life. I think it would be good for her."

"What about your father?" I asked.

"He'll never leave the bush."

"They'll live apart?"

"I think so."

"I'm sorry to hear all that."

"What about you?" she inquired. "What's your story? Are you married?"

"I just got divorced. For the second time." I laughed.

She looked over at me again.

"I always feel like I should apologize or explain the situation when I say that because nobody understands the circumstances but me. I haven't been good at relationships and I haven't been good at making the right choices. The right decisions in my personal life."

"Why not?" she asked.

"This is more than you want to know at this point."

"Tell me."

"I honestly don't know. I think it's more about being afraid of being lonely than wanting to be happy. I think it stems from how I was raised. My father was an orphan of sorts. His mother died in childbirth and his father realized he couldn't raise an infant on his own in the 1930s and began looking for a suitable home for him.

"He knew of a couple who were unable to have children and he contacted them with the proposition: Adopt his child and allow him to see the boy as he grew up so he could be a part of his life in the role of uncle.

"The arrangement worked for everyone. My biological grandfather did a great service for my father, who came to dearly love his adoptive parents who raised him with love, so in the end everyone won.

"But maybe because he was, at least for a short time, an orphan, my father had this sense of longing and seeking that I've never seen in another person except maybe myself. He was a wonderful father to me but his eye was always on the next interaction with nature, and his thirst was unquenchable. Whenever he could during the week he went hunting, fishing, exploring. He had a white-collar job but when he wasn't at work he was always in some field or on some lake somewhere. It's unimaginable in today's world that a person could have such a completely dual life, given the singular requirements of work life nowadays.

"I think the one thing my dad passed along to me was the same instinctual wanderlust, the seeking that never seems to leave me. I think that same sense has been the reason I've gotten married too quickly—as in, I wanted a partner and didn't want to get left behind—but it also led to two divorces. There was always an insurmountable fault with my wives that I couldn't live with. As soon as we settled in I needed to leave, and I couldn't understand why and of course neither could they. In the final analysis, it was all me."

India was still holding her fishing rod, looking at me. Her face was serious. I continued.

"Last month I went to church and the priest was talking about how life is a series of small resurrections. He said that resurrections happen to us continuously and we need to be open to them and understand that they're a part of our life experience in the context of what God is teaching us.

"I've been thinking about that ever since and it's helped me put my life in perspective. I've begun to see my life as a series of small resurrections where I and my partners and even my business, have all grown and been transformed—despite fear, sadness, loneliness, and sometimes betrayal. For example, I'm constantly regretful that I never had kids. But maybe being childless too is a type of resurrection. Maybe that longing has affected me and made me brighter, more alive, and more aware, I don't know." I stopped talking, suddenly aware of how long I'd been going on. But something made me say just one more thing, the thing that was really on my mind.

"Maybe this is my moment. Maybe this is my resurrection."

"Maybe what is your resurrection?" she asked.

"Being here right now with you in the middle of nowhere and feeling so free and unencumbered. I haven't had this feeling for many years, maybe ever."

India looked at me wordlessly. "Let's take a break," she said. We rounded a deep bend in the river and found a downed tree that was the perfect natural bench. We sat and ate a snack from her backpack and filled our bottles with water from the river. The tree lay on a large sandbar that protruded into the stream almost like an arrow, forcing the stream to make a broad turn around it, moving from our right to left. We had 30 yards of a beautiful sand-and-gravel beach dotted with old logs and chunks of coal. It was the perfect spot to rest, and also offered clear views of the surroundings, so no grizzlies could sneak up unannounced.

No wind, no clouds, just unbroken sunshine, and a piercing cobalt blue sky that was unblemished even by jet contrails. It was hot. Occasionally, an eagle would soar overhead, its white head and eight-foot wingspan casting a shadow as it moved up and down and across the stream searching for food. As we sat there mostly in silence, I could hear the sound of the forest around us: alder bushes shaking in the breeze, poplars and cottonwoods creaking as they bent back and forth, their leaves scrubbing the sky, and the myriad of birds, large and small, all singing their soliloquies as the forest rang with its mid-day movement. Whenever we had something to say we had to speak loudly to be heard over the sound of the rushing water, even though we were seated next to each other.

The strong sun bathed us, and India took off her pack and gun, rested her pack against the log, and leaned into it like a backrest, stretching out on a little parcel of sand beside the log. I lay back against the same log not too far from her and looked up at the sky.

Occasionally one of us would get up, wander over to the stream, and cast a lazy line, but we were on break, although India did accidentally catch a silver salmon which took her nearly thirty minutes to land. Afterwards she lay back down beside me and rolled her chest-high waders down to her waist, exposing her bare midriff between the top of the waders and her tee shirt. She pushed her baseball cap down on her head, so the brim covered her eyes.

"Let's swim" she said smiling up at me from under her cap.

"I didn't bring my trunks," I responded

"Me neither, but we have underwear. So when you get as hot as I am, let me know and we can swim, maybe after lunch?"

She rolled her waders farther down her hips to cool off.

Eventually, she started a small fire with kindling and a little coal she had collected from the area around us. As she encouraged the flame it grew hotter, and she carefully added more wood as the flames licked higher into the air, sitting Indian style beside the fire, continuing to build it into the perfect outdoor grill. After about fifteen minutes she took a small frying pan out of her pack and began to cook the Grayling that I had caught earlier. Grayling is the only species of trout legal to kill in this part of Alaska, and their parasite-free meat is so clean and perfect it can be eaten as sushi or cooked.

I sat across from her, looking at her defined jaw and naturally tanned skin, as she continued to work the fire and make our lunch. As she worked she started telling me stories about growing up and living off the grid, how her family survived primarily on moose and dried salmon in the winter and how every single day was a struggle for survival against incredible odds: rain, snow, freezing temperatures that lasted for seven months, making the Lake Smith area of the interior nearly uninhabitable. About the time when she was a young girl and had gone to an outside shed to pick up some frozen meat for dinner and an angry, aggressive bull moose stood between her and the house when she came out of the shed: 1500 pounds of panting, stomping beast ready to charge. How there was no backup for her at that moment—the shed wouldn't stop the beast and she probably couldn't reach the shed before the moose got to her anyway. How if her father hadn't heard her cries for help she could have easily been killed. How her father shot the moose from the house just as it started to approach her and they had meat for the winter.

We sat on the irregular top of the log, both of us facing the stream as a light breeze blew down the river. I'd taken off my waders and sat in my shorts. This was as close as I'd gotten to her since my arrival and I caught a first smell of her: just the slightest hint of soap and musk, something natural and basic that I couldn't place. She picked a filet of cooked Grayling from the fire and placed it on my plate, smiling as she passed it to me along with some potato salad, a healthy portion of fresh baked bread, and an oatmeal cookie. She shifted her position once again so that our arms were nearly touching.

We ate our lunch in silence and watched as the river continued its endless trek toward Cook Inlet. It was September, and the lazy days of summer were reluctantly yielding to the months that would bring harshness to this most beautiful but soon-to-be-barren environment. As I sat there, a passage from Emerson's "Nature" kept repeating itself in my mind, over and over.

"*... to the attentive eye, each moment of the year has its own beauty, and in the same field, it beholds, every hour, a picture which was never seen before, and which shall never be seen again.*"

I felt just like that. Like this was a picture I had never seen before and would never see again. I remember trying to capture every moment of it; to imprint it on my brain.

After lunch she collected our plates and went to the river to clean them and repack the backpack. When she returned, she sat close to me on the log. Her hands were wet from the stream. I waited for the conversation to continue, for the next words to be spoken, but nothing came. Instead she raised her sunglasses to the top of her head, looked at me, and smiled. After a moment she got up and moved toward her pack, re-shouldered the load, picked up her gun, and prepared to move downstream. I could see the taut muscles in her arms and torso. She was a strong, powerful woman.

"You ready?" she asked.

"Yeah."

"Let's go catch some fish."

That afternoon we fished the waterway of life and possibility, and as the day wore on I watched closely as she moved along the river. She had a beautiful casting style, moving with ease as she caught trout after trout, emitting a squeal with each strike. She had perfected roll-casting, a difficult technique used on narrow streams where you cast across the water into small pockets where the trout hide, doing it without back-casting and thus avoiding heavy alder bushes or overhanging trees behind and above you. Without roll-casting many parts of the stream would be unfishable simply because you can't get the fly onto the pool. The idea is to let the rod do the work with just a short twist of the wrist, casting the line rather than the fly. If you can get the technique down you can reach the places where the trout are lying. You can hit the most important water and be rewarded. But it's difficult.

Her roll-cast was seamless and fluid – the line coming off the water and floating toward the pool following an almost imperceptible flick of her wrist. Watching her in the flat sunshine, it seemed almost like I was watching a movie. I could see the line coming off the water, shaking itself free of leftover moisture, arcing into a tight circle, hesitating just a second, then curling back toward the water with the fly dropping on the surface at the last minute, floating down without so much as a splash. People worked a lifetime to perfect this cast, and India probably couldn't tell you how she had learned it or for that matter what the cast was called – it was the byproduct of a lifetime on the water in Alaska.

She watched me use a dry fly, which is not used extensively here because of the abundance of food underneath the surface. Fishermen have a better chance of landing a fish with a salmon egg suspended in water column where trout will come off the bottom to strike without having to surface. I was using a mouse, skittering it along the surface.

Pretty soon she was using a dry fly herself, casting and catching trout on fly patterns she had never heard of, much less ever fished. Her regular fly repertoire consisted of a film canister stuffed with flies that simply worked, could be changed or altered on a whim, or used because the day had become overcast or rain was moving in or it was clearing off. But I suspected she couldn't tell you the name of one of those flies—they were just a handful of flies that worked in every environment on all these waters, based on her experience and feeling.

Watching her, I thought of how fly fishing is like conducting an orchestra, where you manage many instruments individually and when they come together as one you have a movement, you have a symphony. And I thought of a passage on fishing: "*It is really fishermen who experience eternity compressed into a moment.*" That was what I was experiencing now. Eternity compressed into a moment.

We laughed and concentrated, teased and told stories as we moved with ease through the waterway of life and trout. She was outgoing and loud when she was on the stream, laughing continuously as we landed fish after fish. In me, there was a hope that the day would never end. In the late afternoon we took a nap streamside, both of us leaning against a long soft sand bank that overlooked the stream. We finally went for that swim in our underwear, and at last found ourselves standing on the sandbar where the helicopter would pick us up and carry us back to the lodge.

"That went fast," I said as we stood there, wet but drying in the afternoon sun, awaiting our ride home.

"Yeah. Hey, just wondering, what's it like where you live?" she asked.

"You'd be surprised, I think. It's beautiful and rural. I live 38 miles outside the City in west-central New Jersey, where there are rolling hills and beautiful natural hardwood forests. The town I live in, Bernardsville, is small – maybe 7,000 people. It's accessible to the City by train but it also has a rural side which I like. Remember, I'm from Iowa so I need green grass and space. I can mountain bike from my house and fish a free-stone creek twenty minutes away"

"But you commute a long way into New York for work?"

"Yeah. I drive or walk to the train station in town, ride the train for an hour to

Hoboken, then take a ferry across the Hudson River to the lower east side of Manhattan. My office is a five-minute walk from the ferry."

"How long door-to-door?"

"Two hours each way, roughly."

"Why do you live so far from work? Why do you do it at all?"

"It's hard to explain. It was always a dream of mine to live in New York City. I just felt a pull to live there from the time I was a young man. I like the passion, the intensity, the feeling that you're at the center of everything. I've always wanted to be challenged, to go toe-to-toe with success or failure and to look either or maybe both in the eye. "But my existence isn't just big city, like I said. Everyone who isn't familiar with the area thinks it is but it's not. Even with working in New York, I still live in a rural area and I get into the remote woods several times a month. I have a cabin in the Adirondacks, outside of Lake Placid, New York. The cabin is remote, not remote like this, but as remote as you can get anywhere else in the Lower 48. I go there every other weekend. I also have a place in Telluride, Colorado, that's simply magical. It's tucked into the San Juan Mountains of southwest Colorado. I don't get there as much as I used to but it's there."

She looked across at me and smiled. "That sounds great. But I still can't imagine what it must be like to live around and work in New York."

"I understand. Everyone says that but why don't you come visit? You'd be surprised."

She said, "I live in the woods. I don't have a cell phone or a car. I work in Alaska in the summer and then I surf in Mexico or Hawaii in the winter. There's not a part of me that thinks working in a skyscraper everyday completely enclosed without fresh air or access to green space is okay."

"You should come. I think you'd like New York. On some level, it's no different than Alaska. It's impersonal and challenging and there're lots of ways to fail but at the same time, it's got incredible beauty that needs to be seen and experienced to be appreciated. Just like Alaska, but different, obviously. It takes a special breed, just like it takes to live here. We're both frontiersmen, just facing different challenges. Look, by now you know me enough to know how much I love nature. So you know that if there weren't opportunities where I live, I wouldn't live there. It's more complicated than just skyscrapers versus forests, believe me."

Just then the familiar thump of chopper blades could be heard and we watched as the chopper came into view over the pine trees. We moved our gear to the far side of the sandbar so the chopper could have a clear, unobstructed landing area. It settled down onto the sand in another blinding storm of rock and sand, and we quickly loaded our gear into the side storage bins, locked them, and piled in. Almost immediately we became airborne and headed back to the lodge as the sun began to turn slightly orange, indicating the reluctant transition from afternoon to early evening.

CHAPTER THREE

"Then the angel showed me the river of the water of life, bright as crystal, flowing from the throne of God...on either side of the river is the tree of life."

—Revelation 22

I heard a sound outside the cabin. It was early, still dark out. I looked at my watch—it was three-thirty a.m. I turned on my headlamp, swung my legs over the edge of the top bunk, and slowly dropped down onto the floor. Lucy was asleep next to the lower bunk. I pulled back the crude drapes covering the window, and in the pale moonlight I could see a grizzly sow and two cubs moving away from my cabin along the airstrip. They must have come out of the woods between me and the lodge or else come from the river and cut through the property, a route that would take them right past the lodge and my cabin. I got out my .357 and looked again, this time out the front window. I could hear the sow grunting as they continued to walk down the airstrip toward the tundra beyond.

It was cool in the cabin and I stoked the fire in the wood stove. My heart was racing, but after using the bathroom and getting a drink of water I got back into bed and watched as the flames from the fire in the stove cast long shadows along the walls. Eventually I lay back and was soon asleep.

Three hours later I was awakened by the sun pouring through the cabin window just above my head. I lay in the bunkbed listening to the dark-eyed jays, chickadees, thrushes, and swallows sing their sweet good mornings as the sun was waking the world outside.

The cabin was one large room with a bunkbed along the back wall and a small bathroom along the forest side, with a shower, sink, mirror and stool. The rest of the cabin was a fifteen-by-fifteen-foot open room. It had a table and two chairs next to one of the windows that overlooked the landing strip, a crude dresser, and a round table and chair near the window by the front door. In the center of the room a large cast iron wood stove sat on a cotton twill rug, with split wood piled into a metal 5-gallon pail next to the stove. The vaulted ceiling lent the small cabin a feeling of being larger than it was. What it was, was perfect for me.

It was 6:30 a.m. I peered over the edge of the bed. Lucy was beginning to wake up, stretching and yawning as she looked up at me and banged her tail on the floor.

I lay there for a few more moments, then threw back the covers and swung my legs over the edge of the top bunk. I hopped down, petted Lucy, threw three new logs into the fire, and encouraged the fire back to life. I let Lucy out, then rinsed my face at the bathroom sink. The water felt deliciously hot in the cool morning air.

I pulled on some new long underwear, fresh jeans, and a long-sleeved Pearl Jam tee shirt and filled the coffee pot with water and set it on the stove. I opened the blinds and settled into the rocking chair in front of the fire to wait for the coffee and the cabin to heat up.

Someone knocked lightly on the door and without waiting for an answer India opened the door a crack and peered inside smiling, looking like she'd been up for some time.

"Hey, good morning. Anyone awake in here?"

"Not really," I responded. "I haven't had coffee yet, so I don't consider that being awake."

"Me neither. Can I join?"

"Of course."

She swung the door open and came in. She was wearing her usual jeans and tee shirt, with boots instead of flip flops and no hat and no ponytail. Her long hair fell loosely around her shoulders, nearly down to her waist. She brought with her the fragrance and freshness of the outdoors, and a cool breeze of excitement and expectation filled me and made me want to go outside. She sat down on the chair beside me, warming her hands in front of the now-growing fire.

"I want coffee," she said.

"Did you bring breakfast treats?"

"I did. Let's get this coffee made and we'll have breakfast on the front porch."

"Okay. Let me finish getting ready," I said.

I put on my boots, went into the bathroom and quickly brushed my teeth. In the vanity mirror I could see her watching me from her chair, apparently not knowing I could see her in the mirror. The look on her face was warm. She was smiling and she had a curious look to her.

I washed and toweled off my face. By the time I came out of the bathroom the front door was open, sunlight was streaming in, and she was sitting on the porch with our coffees and two fresh-baked cranberry muffins lined up in front of her. I sat down in the other porch chair, the small table between us. I picked up my coffee, leaned back till my chair was resting on its back legs, and looked out at the beautiful morning. "So, what's on the agenda for today?" I asked.

When I turned toward her she was looking out over the landing strip, her hair wrapped in a twist and draped over the front of her right shoulder. She was wearing a V-neck tee shirt today and I could see how tanned her chest was from days on the water.

"Well, if you're up for a little adventure, I was thinking we could go up to a spring creek I know that's probably thirty miles from here. I haven't fished it yet this year but last time I was there it was incredible."

"What's a spring creek?" I asked.

"It's literal—a creek whose source is an actual spring. The average Alaskan spring produces hundreds of gallons of water a minute at its source, and as it travels toward the ocean it joins with other creeks and streams. The spring creek we're going to today if you're up for it, eventually meets the Ann, but that happens way below where we'll go. We would start maybe a mile from the spring itself, in the first area that's big enough to fish. In that spot it's loaded with rainbows. They're a bit smaller because the elevation is higher but incredibly beautiful. The water is icy cold."

"I'm in. But let's relax a bit first and eat our breakfast. This view and this morning are too beautiful to rush."

"Agreed."

She drank her coffee and ate a small portion of her muffin. I could hear her quietly humming a tune that I couldn't place, in a lilting pretty voice. She was sitting in the chair closest to the runway, so as we both looked out onto the expanse before us, she was in my line of sight. She closed her eyes and tilted her head back slightly. The breeze that was softly blowing down the runway would gust occasionally and her long hair would move in the wind, but she seemed unaware, bathing in the morning sunshine and breeze and some distant source of serenity from all appearances. Her fingers tapped her coffee cup in keeping with the nearly inaudible tune, only occasionally opening her eyes to take a sip of coffee and even then, not looking over at me. It was as if she was meditating, connecting to some distant source of serenity. I thought that if Vermeer's *Girl with a Pearl Earring* could come to life, she would look like this. So enigmatic and somehow similar.

We sat there for about thirty minutes quietly drinking our coffee. Then she looked over at me, smiling. It was time to move.

"You didn't eat your breakfast," I said.

"I ate my spiritual breakfast, and the delicious smell of that breeze was better than Maddie's cranberry muffins, which is hard to imagine," she said softly.

"Okay, back to reality. You'd better get your stuff together. Today we're flying the chopper from the pad next to the river, so come down and we'll leave when you get there. The spring creek is a forty-five-minute flight away, so it'll take us longer to get there than normal. I'll bring coffee for the chopper."

"Got it," I said.

I collected the coffee cups from the table, grabbed the remains of the muffins, and went into the cabin while she hurried off to the lodge. I threw my breakfast remains in the small trash can by the door, put her muffin in the backpack, and looked out the window, watching her wrap her long hair in a twist as she walked down the hill with Lucy. Then I quickly gathered my gear and headed for the landing pad by the river. As I rounded the last corner down by the lodge, I could see India loading everything into the side racks on the chopper, then climb in and put on her headset. Caleb was already in place and had started the engines but hadn't yet engaged the rotors. I hurried the last few yards and put my gear in the side rack, climbed into the chopper, and fastened my seat belt.

India handed me my coffee.

"Good morning, kids," Caleb said into our headsets. "Ready to go?"

"Yes," we both responded.

Caleb revved the engine and engaged the rotors and we went quickly into hover, then banked sharply over the river and followed the path of the river for maybe a mile, gaining altitude, then we began to cut across the dense tundra toward the distant Alaska Range. These rides out to the streams were always amazing because of the views you had of the uninhabited and uninhabitable. It was like being on a drone looking down and watching something you weren't supposed to see, something secret. That's what the Alaska wilderness has always meant to me. So unique and wild. It holds a thousand secrets and a million dreams.

Once we were level and on course after twenty minutes or so, Caleb broke the silence. "You guys have enough firepower today? We haven't been up to the spring yet this year but I imagine the wildlife are lively and hungry."

"Yeah," India replied. "I have my 12 gauge with twenty or so shells and Eli has his .357 with plenty of rounds, I'm sure."

"I do," I said. "I'm not one to short-change the life-threatening aspect of this."

There was a mirror hanging in the helicopter in the spot where there would normally be a rear-view mirror in a car, so Caleb could see behind him as he flew. It wasn't used much because a bush helicopter pilot rarely needs to look behind him, and it was askew, nearly sideways, as if it had been turned so someone could check their look in it before getting out of the car. Anyway, it was at an angle that allowed India and me to see each other but Caleb couldn't see us. As we flew, most of my focus was outside the helicopter, but occasionally I caught a glance of her in the mirror. Once I noticed that she was looking at me and smiling. I smiled back and then looked over at her beside me. We were just inches apart and she was blushing.

"Okay, we're just a few minutes out," Caleb said.

We finished our coffee and adjusted our seat belts. I sat more upright, paying attention to where we were now and where we were going to land.

"Where're we going?" I asked.

"Just past that big hill over there is a deep valley and on the north side of that valley is the spring," India answered. "We'll swing over the hill, fly down into the valley, make a sharp turn to the left, and follow the water downstream for a few miles before the stream widens out and we start to see the fishable areas. There's a sandbar just before the first fishable section. We'll set down there."

I leaned forward to get a better view. We gained some altitude to pass over the hill and then we quickly descended into a wide, broad, verdant valley, made an abrupt turn to the left, and began to follow an almost imperceptible stream of water which gained size with every turn until it finally emerged as a full-fledged stream just past the sand bar that India had mentioned.

Caleb circled the landing area to ensure there were no bear or obstructions, then brought the chopper down in the middle of the sandbar. We released our seat belts and slid out the door, opened the outside storage racks and grabbed our gear. Then we moved off to the side so Caleb had an unobstructed takeoff area. We huddled as he gunned the engines, went into hover, and then shot down the stream, gaining altitude as he went.

"Damn, this is remote," I said looking around.

"I told you," she responded. "This is about as remote as you can get in this part of Alaska, which means that this is about as remote as you can get in the entire country. We need to watch for critters. But more importantly, you won't believe the fishing, the scenery, and the solitude."

"Or the company."

She smiled.

We shouldered our packs, got our guns, readied our fly rods, and walked twenty yards downstream to an area where the stream became large enough to fish. She put on a dry fly and I went with a hopper. Both flies were big. Clearly, we had expectations.

"I've made you into a dry fly fisherman," I said.

"We'll see."

As we walked toward the larger portion of the stream, we were quiet. The area was so unique, so remote, that I found it almost distracting or maybe disturbing. The forest edge was just feet from the stream. It was so dense you couldn't see more than a foot or two into the woods, and the terrain had become much steeper. There were small but steep canyons on both sides of us that became larger off in the distance. The smells were different too, fresher and muskier than in the other areas we had fished—the air was lighter and cooler too. The trees were smaller and there were more firs and pines than deciduous trees. The whole area seemed alpine.

"I can see why this is your favorite place." I said. "It's unreal, almost like a different planet. I haven't been to a place like this before. It's magical."

"I know," she said. "When I was a young girl I used to work for Caleb when he was just starting out and we would go on scouting trips to find new water where we could take our fisherman. On those trips we found a world of possibility, both in terms of trout fishing and life. I could tell you stories for days about what I saw on those trips, but nothing struck me like this place. The first time we came here we landed his chopper exactly where we did today, and we were both awestruck by what we found. This was and still is my Oz."

"I think fishing is secondary at this point," I joked.

"Yeah, I'm ok with that too. We can just watch if you want."

"What I want is more time," I said, and I meant it.

We reached a stretch of obviously fishable water. I scanned the area and looked over at her, trying to get a visual clue as to whether we should start fishing. She was staring at me. Then she seemed to snap out of whatever she was thinking or feeling, moved over to me, standing close, and whispered, "in this stretch," she pointed her rod toward the water, "the fish sit beneath the foam line at the edge of the current. Remember this today and don't forget it: *foam is home*. We'll want to keep our flies dead in the center of the foam line. Even though it may seem like the fish can't see the fly through the foam, they can, I promise you."

"Foam is home," I said.

"The fish here are smaller and lazier than in the other place we fished. They sit just off to the side of the channel and wait for food. Cast your fly upstream and let it flow down through the foam line and make sure to strip your line as it comes toward us – they'll hit hard and quick and you can't have any slack line or you'll miss the strike."

"Ok," I said. "Foam is home. You want to take the upstream side today or do you want me too?"

"You take it. Let's see how your dry flies work today. We also need to be more quiet streamside today—these fish are leader shy and shy of shadows and movement and noise on and near the stream, and for sure they haven't seen a human before. Pay attention."

I moved to the upstream position and she followed behind me, repeating our strategy of yesterday. Me casting upstream and doing a float down to even to where I was, then recovering the line and repeating the process, walking just a few steps upstream with each cast.

I caught a fish on the second cast and she did too. This was beyond description.

After we landed the second fish she looked over and said to me abruptly, as if this was something she had been thinking about for a while, "How old are you?"

"Too old for you most probably."

"I like older men," she said as she sent a cast upstream from where we were standing.

Just then her rod bent double and she squealed with delight.

"Big one!" she screamed. "Rainbow!"

The fish was large – larger than what she had told me was here and what we had already caught. I helped her land it softly on the edge of the stream, then held the net in the water with the fish still in it. It was beautiful. The rainbow stripe on its side was so pronounced it looked like it was painted on or something out of a child's coloring book. She reeled in her line behind me, then bent to see the fish.

"Damn," I said. "That is one beautiful fish. Perfection."

"I was lucky to catch him. My mind was wandering when he hit, just like I told you not to let happen."

"Do as I say, not as I do, huh?"

We released the fish, organized ourselves after the catch, and walked back up to a spot just beyond where she caught the rainbow. At this point the stream was still small, maybe twenty feet across, and the canyon walls rising on either side of it were getting closer to the water. We were approaching an area that looked like we would have maybe fifteen feet on either side of the water to cast without catching the canyon walls. It was almost as if we were walking into a box canyon. It looked exciting.

"Shall we have some coffee?" she asked.

We had only been on the water for a half hour and I was surprised by the quick break.

"Sure."

We settled on a small flat sandbar between the water and a towering canyon, took off our packs, and lay our rods against some driftwood. She unpacked the thermos, poured two steaming cups of coffee, and handed one to me, the steam rolling off the cups in the cool morning air. We sat on a large log. The morning was idyllic. Blue skies, a light breeze, temperatures in the high 50s, and abundant sunshine.

She looked over after we were settled.

"So, do you have any kids?"

"No. I missed that boat. Regrettably."

"How come?"

"I don't know. It wasn't intentional, I wanted kids. It just never happened. I guess I wasn't with one woman long enough to move to that phase."

She looked off into the distance. Downstream. A lock of hair that had escaped from her rubber band that held her ponytail in place, and fell across the side of her face. She gently moved it behind her ear then flipped the rest of her hair behind her, and I could see her taking in the view around us, studying the river. I watched her intently as she looked up and down the stream and into the water at something visible to no one else, her hazel eyes throwing off copper sparks from the reflection of the water. I suspected that what she was seeing in the river wasn't trout.

"What do you see in that water?" I asked.

Without looking over at me or raising her gaze from the river, she said. "The same thing I always see—grace and truth and hope, I guess.

"I was raised on water and on rivers in particular, and I've come to believe in them. It's hard to put into words, but Christians have Jesus Christ and maybe I do too, but for me He's those swirling pools of emerald green right there, all linked together on a trip to everlasting life. Water is my ancestral home. It's what keeps me warm and calm and centered. When I get conflicted or upset I go back to it and it finds a way to center my heart and tell me everything will be okay. I can't take my eyes off it and I don't want to leave its side. "

She moved to face me.

"I'm sorry. I haven't shared that before."

"It's beautiful. I'm glad you did."

"It's just that rivers give us so much. They give us a map; we just have to be patient enough to follow it and listen and watch. The native people have always gotten the river connection right."

Suddenly she moved her head and cocked it to one side, then turned toward me.

"Do you hear that?" she asked.

"What?" I said.

"It sounds like a helicopter in the distance."

I listened intently and through the light breeze I could just make out the distant, faint thump-thump of what sounded like a helicopter. It seemed to be coming our way but still a long way off. As we sat there listening the sound grew louder.

"Caleb never comes out during the day—ever—and there wouldn't be another helicopter anywhere close to us. Unless by some remote chance it's the Forest Service."

From the sound of it, the helicopter was following our flight path in: paralleling the stream from a long way off, then sounding as if it were flying over the hill and turning sharply down into the riverbed. We couldn't see it but it was clearly coming our way now, the sound getting louder by the second.

"It's Caleb or Dave," she said. "There's no way anyone else would know of this area. Something must be up."

In seconds the helicopter roared around the last bend, then settled down on the sandbar where Caleb had dropped us off no more than an hour earlier. We set down our coffee, left everything where it was, and starting walking quickly back to the helicopter. Its rotors were slowing and the engine was shut off as we got closer.

The door opened and Caleb emerged. He looked serious, walking toward us with purpose.

"Hey guys," he said. "India, I'm sorry to say there's an issue with your mom – she took a bad fall and is hurt from that. She's also having what appears to be some seizures. Jacob called and said you need to get over there as soon as possible."

"Oh my God," India said. "Let's get out of here."

"I'll get the gear," I said. I turned and ran the fifty yards back to where we had been sitting. I put everything back in the pack, shouldered the load, picked up the gun and our rods, and ran back to the chopper. Caleb was standing outside it waiting for me so we could stash the gear. India was already inside the helicopter waiting for us with her headphones on. I ran around and got inside beside her and Caleb opened his door and got in. We buckled our belts and within a few seconds he fired up the engines and we went into a quick hover, then he yanked the collective and we pulled up off the sandbar and shot off downstream. India asked Caleb to recall everything that Jacob had said, and he repeated what he had said before. After that we were quiet for nearly the entire ride back.

Caleb broke the silence as we approached camp. "Ok, how do you want to do this, India? We're going to have to take the plane over to your parents' house. It's too far for the chopper. I can get the plane ready now while you pack. Do you want to leave immediately? Your brother Jacob seemed to think you need to get there ASAP."

"Let me pack a bag and change clothes and I'll meet you at the plane. Give me fifteen minutes."

She looked over at me.

"Will you come?"

I was shocked. I'd been too caught up in the intensity of the moment to even think about going, but if I had thought about it I would have assumed she would go alone.

"Sure," I replied instinctively.

"Ok, you do the same—pack a bag quickly and meet us at the plane. I have no idea what's happening over there so this could be uncomfortable and stressful. I think I could use your help but I don't want to put you in a bad position. You sure you're in?"

"I am. Meet you at the plane."

Caleb looked over at me with concerned eyes.

CHAPTER FOUR

*"Peace is the beauty of life. It is sunshine...
the togetherness of a family. It is the advancement
of man, the victory of a just cause, the triumph
of truth."*

—Menachem Begin

India and I jumped out of the helicopter as soon as Caleb cut the engines. I unloaded the gear and took India's backpack and my rod and started running up the hill to my cabin to change and get my gear. I stopped at the lodge and ran up the stairs, opened the screen door, and dropped India's pack on the floor. Maddie was standing in the kitchen and turned when she heard the door open.

"What's going on?"

"We're heading over to India's parents' house to see what's happening. Apparently, her mom's had an accident. Can you please unpack her backpack?"

"Of course. I heard about her mom from Caleb. Keep us posted on everything."

I left the lodge and ran up the hill toward the runway and my cabin. Caleb was some distance behind me but hurrying as well. I reached the top of the rise and ran the few remaining yards over to my cabin. I took off my waders on the porch and went inside to pack. I had no idea how long I was going to be gone or where I was going, but I was happy to be asked to go along. I couldn't believe she'd asked me to come.

I threw some warmer clothes, rain gear, and toiletries into my backpack, quickly washed my hands and ran a razor over my face, grabbed a down coat from the hooks by the front door, and headed out the door. The plane was parked on the runway, 35 yards from my front door. Caleb had already taken the tie-downs from the wings and was doing his flight pre-check. The engine cowling was up and he was checking the oil when I got there.

"I'll throw my stuff in the backseat. What can I help with?" I asked.

"Nothing, we're good."

I tossed my backpack and jackets into the plane's backseat. India would sit in the front with Caleb.

"Hey, I want to talk to you for a second," Caleb said. He closed the engine cowling, latched it, and walked around the front of the plane to where I was standing. He glanced nervously down the airstrip toward the lodge.

"What's up?" I said.

"This is all happening so fast, but I wanted to give you some friendly advice about India's family."

"Okay."

"Look, people who come to Alaska are a strange lot. I'm no exception, but India's family is unique—especially her father. Her mom's an angel, but her dad isn't. He's an extremist, a far-right guy who's suspicious of the government and all form of regulation. He's also suspicious and unfriendly to almost everyone he doesn't know and many he does. You don't want to cross him. He's a guy who doesn't trust

43

anyone outside of his family and is extremely protective of them. I've known him for the better part of 25 years, and I don't trust him, like him, or want to be around him, but I make it my business to stay on his good side. That way, he looks at me as a friend and I keep close enough to him to know what he's up to. I never turn my back on him, and you shouldn't either. He also has a bit of a consumption problem, so when booze is present, which it will be, tread even lighter, and I'm not kidding.

"I'm always amazed at how well balanced the kids turned out despite him—I think that's where their mom comes in. But anyway, I'm surprised India asked you to go. I think that says a ton about you and how she feels about you, but you need to watch yourself around him. Give him a few beers and you better watch your back because he can turn on you in an instant. Even without the beers, he's an asshole handful. I don't have any idea what's going on over there, but India's brother Jacob wouldn't have called if it wasn't serious. Watch yourself and keep me posted. I'll check my email a bit more closely over the next few days. I know they have a computer that's connected to a satellite and they can email. Use it. I'll come get you when things clear up. One other thing, the weather forecast for the next few days is horrible. I'll get there when I can, but don't expect me for at least a couple days at the earliest."

At that moment India came over the rise and headed toward the plane with a backpack slung over her shoulder. I went over grabbed her gear and stowed her stuff in the back with mine.

"Are we ready?" I asked India.

"Let's get out of here," she said.

I moved the front seat forward, climbed into the back, fastened my seatbelt, and grabbed the pair of headphones beside my seat. Once I was settled India climbed into the front and did the same. Caleb was still locking up the outside of the plane.

The headphones were live.

"Hey," I heard India say through mine.

"Hey."

"Thanks for going with me. I don't know what's going on over there but I'm glad to have you with me."

"My pleasure."

"My family can be crazy—well, not my family, but my dad. We didn't have any time to talk about this. He has a unique perspective on things, so I want you to know that. I'm sorry to put you in the middle here. Maybe this isn't the best idea, but I guess we're past the point of no return?"

"I'm good with people. I'm just here to help you. I won't get in the way and maybe I can lend a hand."

Caleb jumped into the pilot's seat and put on his headphones.

"You guys ready?" he asked.

"Yes"

"Ok, let's go."

He pushed the starter and the engine coughed and sputtered to a start. The entire plane shuddered, then settled into a smooth idle. We sat there for a couple of minutes while Caleb worked through his pre-flight checklists. He finally looked around in all directions then gave the engine some gas and the plane moved slowly out of the grass parking spot on the edge of runway and began to taxi toward the other end of the strip, lurching and pitching as it navigated the uneven runway.

I knew that, given the wind today, we would take off in the direction of my cabin and the lodge. As we reached the end of the runway, Caleb made a tight U-turn and lined up for take-off. He stopped the plane to check the instruments one last time. Then he looked at both of us as if to check in and gunned the engine. We moved quickly down the runway, hitting the same rough spots and pitching from side to side, then lifted off at about the spot where the plane had just been parked. We leveled off about ten minutes after takeoff and began a sweeping turn to the left.

It seemed like something needed to be said to bring us back to some degree of normalcy.

"So, how far is it and where do we land," I asked.

"It's about an hour and twenty minute flight and we can land close to my family's house. We have an airstrip just a hundred yards or so from the house, not unlike the set up at Caleb's place. It's flat over there so we don't have to dodge anything. Fairly straightforward."

"Usually," Caleb said and smiled over at India.

"Yeah, usually," she said. "Sometimes if it's been raining a while and the airstrip is muddy it's not so easy."

"Okay, now, just so we know what's going to happen from a logistics standpoint, send me an email everyday so I know what's happening and when to come pick you up," Caleb said. "Also, as I just told Eli, the weather isn't looking good for the next few days so it may be a while before I can get over."

"Sounds good. I can also call you on the satellite phone if need be," India replied. "And thanks for doing this. I know it's an unexpected trip and you have another fisherman staying at the lodge, so sorry about that. And sorry about taking one of your fishermen with me."

"This guy here isn't much of a fisherman so it's no biggie," Caleb said, smiling at me in the rearview mirror.

"True," she said. "He may have other redeeming qualities, although I've always felt that fishing is the only quality that matters in a man."

"Nice vacation," I said. "I get pulled off a stream, thrown into the backseat of a shitty plane, and then get made fun of."

We got quiet again and the flight got a bit bumpy. We'd been in the air about forty minutes and I assumed we were over halfway there. I couldn't see the expression on their faces so I had no idea what either of them was thinking. Every so often India looked back at me and smiled.

"Ok guys, we're about ten minutes out," Caleb finally said.

We were over Lake Smith, located at the confluence of the Tobler and Antuit rivers. The terrain was flatter here than where we had just come from and there was water everywhere. So, this was where she was from, I thought.

"Do you see where those two rivers come together up there, just past that big bend in the river below us?" India asked.

"Yeah, I see that." I said, moving forward in my seat so I could look over the front cowling of the plane.

"That's where we're heading. We'll cross over that confluence and then make a wide right turn to line up with the runway. You ready?" she asked, looking back at me again.

"Yes."

Caleb started slowly descending, and at the confluence of the two rivers we made a wide right turn and I could see a clearing up ahead.

"Is that it over there?" I asked, pointing to the clearing.

"Yeah. You can't really see the house from here but that's the landing strip."

Caleb made a couple of adjustments to our speed and altitude, then finally we were lined up and descending fast. At 100 yards out he reduced power almost to idle speed and we began softly floating toward the strip. I sat up in my seat, surveying the surrounding area. Now I could see the house. It was much nicer and larger than what I'd imagined, with beautifully manicured gardens, a metal roof, newly painted green siding, and a graceful lawn that must have been at least five acres square. We were landing directly over the vegetable garden. We were so close to it I could see that it was still bearing some lingering squash, tomatoes, and cabbage.

As we touched down on the soft dirt, I looked over at the house and saw a young man and woman emerge and head over toward the airstrip. They were both tall and rail thin. The boy was maybe in his mid twenties; the girl looked younger, like she was in her early twenties or late teens. They were wearing jeans and tee-shirts and both had on boots.

"That's my brother and sister. Jacob and Ruth," India said.

I remembered the name Jacob from earlier in the day. Both names sounded biblical. It made me wonder if India's father was also a religious fundamentalist. If so, that would be in keeping with his extremism, whatever that meant. It also made me wonder about India's name—so different, so much more exotic, than the names Jacob and Ruth. Was that her mother's choice? Was India born before her father and maybe her mother too became fundamentalists?

Caleb maneuvered the plane to a siding near the end of the runway and shut down the engine. We took off our headphones and India opened her door, jumped down, and embraced her brother and sister who had run up to the plane. I slid the front seat forward, put on my backpack and grabbed India's and stepped out of the plane onto the runway. Both Jacob and Ruth looked at me, a bit surprised.

"This is Eli. He's up fishing for the week and we've spent some great time together, so I asked him to come with me," India explained.

"Hi." I said extending my hand to each of them. They both shook enthusiastically.

Caleb spoke up from the plane.

"Hi Jacob, Hi Ruth. If you guys are all set, I'll be on my way."

Jacob and Ruth returned the pleasantries and India shut the passenger door.

"Thanks Caleb," India said.

"My pleasure. Remember the daily email and give my regards to your parents."

"Will do both."

Caleb looked over at me seriously one more time before he started the engine. Then he gave me a short smile and a thumbs up.

We all moved to the grass alongside the runway as Caleb started the engine, taxied back down the runway, turned, gunned the engine, and was airborne by the time he got to where we were standing.

CHAPTER FIVE

"Our truest life is when we are in dreams, awake."

—Henry David Thoreau

I picked up our gear and we started walking slowly towards the house. Ruth spoke first.

"India, it's bad. Yesterday Mom seemed a bit disoriented in the afternoon, just before dinner. Jacob and I noticed something but figured she was just tired. At around five when she was in the kitchen by herself, we heard a crash and rushed in to find that she had taken a bad fall. I mean *bad*. She fell holding a large urn of butter she'd just churned, almost the size and weight of a bowling ball. From what I can tell she hit her shoulder hard on the edge of the counter and then hit her head on the floor. She was unconscious. It took several minutes for her to come to and she's been disoriented and very confused ever since. I think she may have had a stroke which caused her to lose her balance and I'm fairly certain she also broke her shoulder, when she hit the counter."

"We have to get her to an emergency room now," India said.

"It's not going to be that simple," Jacob said. "Dad's on a roll and doesn't want to take her in. He thinks she just needs to rest and that she bruised her shoulder. I assure you, it's way worse than that. She's had a stroke and we need to get her out of here. This is a bad time for his grandstanding. I think her life's in jeopardy. That's why I called you."

We kept walking towards the house. I felt suddenly uncomfortable. I had no idea how this was going to play out, but more importantly I could see it was a mistake to plant myself in the middle of a major family squabble with a wild man at the helm.

We got to the house and walked up the steps, me bringing up the rear, India in front. Her father was standing on the other side of the door. He was a monster of a man. At least 6 foot 4 and built like a house, with a beard to match and forearms the size of tree trunks. He greeted her with a bear hug and swung her off her feet.

"My baby girl! Now why in the world would you come back here when you've got a job to do?"

"Hi Dad. Anytime my mom or dad becomes disoriented, falls and maybe breaks a bone, I'm going to come to help. Where's Mom?"

"She's upstairs in bed. Let her sleep."

He looked around and saw a new face in the crowd.

India quickly intervened.

"Dad, this is my friend Eli. I asked him to come with me. We've been fishing together over at Caleb's place this week."

He stared at me and frowned.

"Where you from?" he asked gruffly. He was massive in every way and his voice

51

carried as far as his outsized ego.

"New York now but originally from Iowa." I said, throwing in Iowa so he might think I was a farm kid and thus have better credentials.

"New York, what a piece of shit that must be," he said.

"Dad, I'm going up to see Mom." India said. She began to climb the steps to the second floor of the house.

I stood in the entryway with our packs, feeling completely uncomfortable. Finally Ruth looked at me and smiled.

"Eli, please come in and set those packs down. Would you like some tea or water?"

"Water would be great, thanks." I followed Ruth into the living room and set the packs in a chair. The living room was large and modern with a split stone fireplace that occupied the entire length of the far side of the room. Above the fireplace was a huge Moose head and I wondered about the story behind it. The balance of the room was typically furnished with two large sectional sofas and easy chairs situated in a u-shape around the fireplace hearth. The back of the room looked out onto the rear yard through a bay window that was magnificent, running nearly the entire rear of the house. Jacob and his father were still standing in the entryway.

The dad looked over at me and glowered. "How long are you going to stay? Overnight?"

"I'm not sure what the plan is. Seems like an overnight might be safe to assume though."

"Don't get too comfortable. You can take your gear downstairs to the guest room and Jacob will take India's stuff up to her room. Show him where the basement is, Jacob. This ain't any fancy New York City hotel so you'll be roughing it."

"I'm comfortable anywhere."

Jacob gave me a nod and I grabbed my pack and followed him downstairs into the basement. I put my pack on a cot in the corner and looked around. It was a typical basement, a storage place for Christmas ornaments and boxes of memories, with a washer and dryer and a small table next to the cot in the corner. That area appeared to function as the guest room.

Jacob stood awkwardly off to the side, swaying from foot to foot. He was silent but I got the impression something needed to be said. He was as tall as his father but he hadn't grown into his frame. Just like his sister, he had brown hair and hazel eyes. His hair was long – shoulder length and he wore a trucker hat with a fishing logo. He wore rough brown boots and had long gangly arms that were muscular. He seemed unsure about the interaction with me.

"I'm sorry about your mom, Jacob. I'm just here to help in any way possible. I know your sister makes good decisions so we'll get a game plan in place and I'm sure everything will be fine in a few days."

"You don't know my dad. He thinks Mom just bruised her shoulder and she's disoriented because she's tired. She's not tired—she's hurt and hurting and I'm scared shitless. He nearly killed me when I called over to Caleb's. He's not a rational man."

I gave him a long look. He was completely freaked out which in turn freaked me out.

"I understand," I finally said. "Let's go upstairs and see what's up, see what India's feeling about this."

"Okay, but you can't discuss getting Mom out of here in front of Dad. Or, I guess you can, but it won't go well. We all need to be careful."

"I'm getting the picture," I said. "Let's play it by ear. Come on." We turned and walked back toward the stairs and I put my arm around his shoulder.

When we emerged into the kitchen Ruth was sitting alone at the table in front of a picture window. The window provided a sweeping view of the surrounding wilderness and the Tobler river 200 yards away, at the far side of a stretch of lawn. Given the otherwise almost impenetrable forest that was unbroken for miles flying in, I couldn't imagine what it must have taken to clear a lawn of this size. I looked around the room. Just as with the outside, the interior of the house was nicer and more modern than what I had anticipated. The kitchen itself was unremarkable from any other modern kitchen – double sink, granite countertops, center island with gas range and oven and two seating areas – one, a island that extended from the end of the kitchen that wrapped the kitchen in an "L" shape, and the other a small seating area that was nestled in a bay window at the other end of the space.

Before we could say anything to Ruth, we heard footsteps coming down from the second floor. Ruth jumped up and she and Jacob rushed around the corner to the hallway to meet India. I followed.

"How is she?" Ruth asked.

"She's resting, but she needs to get to a hospital. She's completely disoriented but not from the fall, and I would say her shoulder's broken. She's in a lot of pain. I also think she has a slight fever."

India gave me a troubled look. No tears, but I saw in her eyes the kind of pain you recognize. Deeper than what brings tears. I went over and put one arm around her shoulders. She turned and hugged me tightly. Ruth and Jacob stood off to the side, watching. Their Dad had left. I could hear sounds coming from what must have been the shop, because it sounded like someone was doing vehicle repair, so I assumed he went out there.

"Where's Dad?" India asked Ruth and Jacob?

"He went out to the shop," Jacob said.

India looked at me. "Let's get some fresh air."

"Of course. I want to walk this beautiful property. We need to let your sister catch her breath and make a plan," I said to Ruth and Jacob.

I picked up my jacket from the back of the chair as we moved toward the front door. India looked back at Jacob and Ruth.

"Ruth, can you get Mom some fresh water and a towel moistened with cool water, please? Let's see if we can get that fever down."

It was midafternoon and the temperature had dropped significantly since our arrival. Clouds had moved in and it was windy. It looked like rain later tonight. We walked down the front steps onto the lawn and kept walking straight toward the river, 200 yards directly in front of the house. The lawn was manicured all the way to the river. To the right was more yard that ended abruptly in a dense forest about 75 yards away, and to the left was more expanse of lawn ending in a gravel driveway that led to a large shop building. The shop's doors were open and the lights were on. I saw several large trucks, two ATV's, and two snowmobiles inside. I caught a glimpse of India's dad working on one of the trucks as we made our way toward the river.

"Mom's bad," India said. "If we don't get her out of here in the next day or so, I don't think she's going to make it. She's barely conscious and her shoulder is broken. We need a plan, and I'm sorry to say this, but you need to help me."

"Of course. That's why I'm here. But I can't give you much advice in terms of how we're going to convince your dad."

"We'll make one try of it tonight at dinner. If that isn't successful, we're going to have to get her out either despite him or around him."

"Look, I don't know your family dynamics, but from what I'm feeling so far, I don't think we have the means to get her out of here if your father doesn't want her to go. It seems like it would take a lot to get around him."

"Or a fantastic plan that makes it happen without him knowing," she said.

"I don't think that's practical, frankly," I said.

"Why not?"

"To a certain extent, we're prisoners here – not literally, but figuratively. There's no way we can do anything, at least as far as I can see, that he wouldn't be able to smell out. And we're all under the same roof, there are no practical transportation options in or out of here and there's nobody we can rely on, no neighbors or friends who could drop in to help, right"? I'm not against the idea that we need to get her out of here, but I don't see anything slapping me in the face that makes an alternative plan reasonable that he isn't a part of."

"I suppose. But I'm going to try to think of something."

We walked the length of the lawn to the banks of the river. The weather was rapidly getting worse, cold and windy, and now it was starting to rain. The Tobler River was in full rage. It was roaring so loudly, I could barely hear anything India was saying. It looked like a flood. I could see massive trees being swept past in the tea-brown water that was foaming and in a full maddening torment.

We moved away from the water to a spot under some trees where it was a little quieter and we could hear each other speak. "The other bad news is that the weather forecast for the next few days is horrible," India said. "I checked the weather radio when I was upstairs with my mother. Rain every day with gale-force winds and cold temperatures. There are advisories for everything—high wind, rain, hail, snow in the high country and high tide warnings for the coast. Highs in the low 50s, with overnight lows in the 40s which will complicate everything we need to do because the only way out of here is by boat or airplane.

I'm not sure Caleb or anyone else could get a plane in here, and a boat is a problem because it's a rough ride and it would be impossible to make her comfortable."

"What about the trucks I saw in the shop?" I asked.

"Those are work trucks that were boated in years ago. They're used to manage the homestead. They work like a charm for that but there are no roads in or out of here, so they're useless for our mission. You couldn't drive five feet into the forests around here – they're impenetrable."

We continued walking, circling the property. We walked south along the river where the lawn met the grass runway, then turned and walked the length of the runway. "Your place is so much nicer than I envisioned. From your descriptions of not having electricity or heat or phones, I guess I thought I was heading to a small dark cabin. This is anything but that," I said.

"The one thing I give my dad credit for is his resourcefulness. He built everything you see by hand and he did it all for us and Mom. He's had 25 years to get our place to this point, and he would go to any lengths to keep us comfortable. So our experience growing up off the grid was in many ways better than what kids who live in town have, despite our lack of services. We just didn't have any friends – our friends and family were the same. That was the most difficult sometimes."

We were approaching the shop from the rear. I could hear tools clanging inside a large metal shed.

As we came to the front of the shop, India looked over at me. I wasn't sure if we were going into the house or the shop. "Let's chat with Dad for a second."

"Really? You really want to engage him now?"

"Look, I've got to connect with him. The objective is to get Mom out of here, and if he's the one standing in the way, I have to do whatever it takes to either make him an ally in that effort or keep him from being suspicious if we're going to find a way around him. Stay with me on this, I know my dad." She reached over and squeezed my hand.

We walked around the metal pole building. The large shop doors were still open and lights were on inside it. India's father was bending over the engine of one of the trucks, his back to us. I saw three beer cans on a shelf near him with another one sitting on the frame of the truck.

"Hi Dad," India said. "What's going on?"

"Trying to fix this goddamn alternator," he said without looking up.

"Need some help?" she asked.

"No. What are you doing out here in this weather?" He finally straightened and looked up. He frowned when he saw me beside India.

"We're taking a walk and just getting some fresh air. Trying to think about what's best for Mom. I think I know how you feel about this but I'm pretty sure she needs to see a doctor as soon as possible. Got any ideas on how we can get her out of here in the shape she's in?"

"Bullshit," he said. "I've known that woman for 35 years and she's tough as nails. She'll get some rest and in a couple days she'll recover. Those shithead doctors in Anchorage can't do anything for her that we can't do here. Best thing for her is to stay put in her own bed and get some rest."

I could detect the faintest slur in his words. He was agitated. He shifted from foot to foot as he spoke, rocking back and forth. His face was flushed and his eyes were bloodshot.

"Dad, forget her shoulder. She's having trouble focusing on anything and when she's awake she's out of it. I think she's had a stroke. For God's sake, she can't even sit on the toilet without assistance, let alone get into the bathroom. What are you missing here?"

"For Christ's sake. Did you come all the way over here to spread this kind of bull crap? Is your boyfriend a doctor? She's staying here. And don't talk to Ruth or Jacob about this. We're doing just fine. Go back to Caleb's place and finish your work before this gets bad for all of us."

"Dad, I'm not trying to cause you any stress. This has nothing to do with Eli. This is Mom we're talking about. We need to make sure she gets the best care possible, and I don't think it would hurt to have her see a doctor. What if we get Doc Thompson to fly out – would that work?"

He threw his wrench hard onto the concrete floor. "I've got to finish replacing this fucking alternator before dinner. Your mom isn't going anywhere, end of story."

And just like that, the conversation was over. He bent back over the front of the truck as we left for the house.

Over her shoulder India called, "Dinner should be ready in an hour or so." He didn't respond.

At the house we walked up three steps, went through the backdoor, and stepped into the mud room lined with all manner of work clothes, overalls, boots, hats and gloves. A washer and dryer stood against one wall and the linoleum floor was covered with a large woven rug. The room was warm, well lighted, and inviting. We took off our wet jackets and hung them on coat hooks that ran the length of the left hand wall, kicked our boots onto a rubber mat, then walked into the family room. Ruth was sitting in a wooden rocking chair in front of a roaring fire.

"Ruth," India said, "we're going to check-in on Mom and then we can start dinner. Eli, it would be helpful to me if you could see my mom. I'd like to have your eyes on this to see if you agree with what I see. Maybe I'm not reading this right."

"Okay."

"Are you alright?" India said to Ruth.

Ruth got up and came over to us, her eyes welling with tears. She put her arms around India and the two of them hugged and quietly sobbed. I stood off to the side wondering where Jacob was and how long we had before their dad came storming into the house. India stepped back from Ruth and said, "This is going to be all right, Ruth, but we'll need your help. Trust me on this but get ready."

India motioned me over to the staircase and we climbed to the second floor. At the landing we turned right and walked down the length of the hall, past two rooms opposite each other. There were no lights on anywhere. We said nothing and walked on tiptoes as we approached the last bedroom, on the right. I was concerned about what shape we'd find India's mom in, but much more concerned about what would happen if her dad saw both of us up here checking on her. He wouldn't tolerate me being even close to this situation or on the second floor of his house.

India peered into the room, smiled softly, and said quietly, "Hi Mom, how are you doing?" She walked further into the room, her face slightly illuminated by light from a small dim lamp on a bureau beside the bed. I followed. India's mother was leaning against a stack of pillows, a pained expression on her face. I saw immediately that she was very pretty, despite how ill she looked. She had dark auburn hair just like India's and probably just as long. Maybe down to her waist, although I couldn't see because she was leaning back and partly under the covers. Her skin was deeply tanned and her eyes were deep blue. On the bedside table, next to the lamp, was a radio, a bottle of water, a washcloth, and a pill bottle. She looked up at us and smiled weakly as we approached the bed.

"Hi sweetie," she mumbled.

"Mom, this is Eli. He's a good friend of mine. We were fishing together over at Caleb's this week."

"Hi," I said. "It's so nice to meet you. I'm sorry you aren't feeling well."

"Nice to meet you too," she whispered. She laid her head back on the pillow, looked from one to the other of us, and appeared to pass out, her breathing shallow and labored as she went limp against the pillows. Her cheeks were sunken and she looked jaundiced.

India felt her forehead. "She's still got a fever." She softly wiped her mother's brow and lips with the washcloth that was sitting on the bedside table. "Come here," she said. I walked closer to the bedside as India pulled back her Mom's nightgown from her left shoulder. There was a huge lump where her shoulder and collarbone met, and the entire area was deeply bruised, nearly black with purple and yellow splotches. It was an angry wound. I couldn't imagine how much something like that must hurt.

"Oh, not good. I can't tell if it's the shoulder or collarbone. I'm no doctor, but somethings broken and I hope it's just one thing that's broken. She needs to get out of here."

India pulled the gown back into place, turned off the light, and motioned for us to go back outside.

"Luckily we had some strong pain relievers from when Dad cut off his the end of his finger a few years ago," she said quietly in the hallway. "He wouldn't go to the doctor, of course, but I called one and got the prescriptions flown here. He quit taking them almost immediately, and we kept the bottle. It's the only thing keeping her comfortable. But they won't last long. We need a plan."

"I know," I said.

"Dinner won't be fun," she whispered, abruptly changing the subject. "It's normally only tolerable because Mom keeps him in check and if she doesn't I try to. He rarely messes with me for some reason, but on some topics there's no persuading him or talking him down or out of something and my stomach tells me this is one of those times. I'd be shocked if he agrees to get her out of here despite how obvious it is that she needs to get to a hospital."

"What do you want me to do?" I asked.

"Think about a plan. We need to set up some sort of diversion to keep him focused on that while we get her out of the house and onto something that can get her to Anchorage. Maybe you walk down by the river while we're getting dinner ready and call Caleb and see if he can get in here sometime tomorrow. Your cell might work down there, but if not, I'll give you the satellite phone—you can get through to him on that."

"Look, I took flying lessons a few years ago. I got to the point where I did my solo flight but stopped after that because I couldn't spare the time. The point is, given the weather, I don't think there's a snowball's chance in hell that Caleb can get in here. And even if he could, how does your dad not hear that? Our diversion would have to take him a considerable distance away for him not to hear the plane and come running back."

She chewed the side of her lip and concentrated. We were still standing in the hallway outside her mom's room, whispering as we spoke.

"Wait, what about Caleb's helicopters? They can fly in any weather and are still loud but quieter than a plane," she said.

"Same problem." I said. Your father would hear it coming and be back here in a flash and the helicopters Caleb flies don't have the range to come over here and then fly to Anchorage without refueling. The ceiling is too low for them anyway, it's barely above the trees."

"One other option," India said, still whispering in the hallway. "The Buckleys, our neighbors to the west, have a grass runway. I'm sure that's better than our dirt one which is now nothing but mud with all this rain. Conceivably, a plane could land in the rain over there. If Caleb landed there it could be heard from here but barely, and it wouldn't be unusual because the Buckleys fly in and out several times a week during the season. My dad wouldn't be alarmed by that. Their homestead is roughly four miles away and there's an old logging trail between our place and theirs. Jacob told me last week that they went back to Anchorage for the season, so I think we'd have the place to ourselves to stage our escape, and I doubt Dad knows they're gone for the season."

She gave me an intense, expecting look, as if what she was about to say was crazy. "The other option is that I call the Buckleys in Anchorage and explain the situation and you go over and fly us out in their plane. It's a Cessna, if I recall correctly. They have two planes and always leave one at their house here."

"You're shitting me," I said. "It's delusional. I haven't flown in years and never got my license, remember? I soloed, but that hardly qualifies me to fly in remote Alaska in one of the worst storms of the summer. I appreciate the confidence you have in me, but I thought we were trying to save your mom, not kill her and us at the same time."

"I admit it's not ideal. But what if it's our only shot of getting out of here? I hate to say it, but that's the truth. You may have to man up," She said.

"How do I go from harmlessly being on vacation for some relaxing fly-fishing to stealing an airplane and running from a man three times my size with an arsenal of weapons, to flying the plane in gale force winds with a very sick woman and three children on board?"

"I would suggest next time you be more careful who you choose to associate with and help," she said, smiling for the first time in a while. "And you wouldn't be stealing the plane, unless of course I can't get ahold of the owners. And, I'm not a child."

"And when is it that you want to pull off this caper?" I asked.

"If Dad won't go along with the rational course, then it has to be tomorrow."

"For the record, I think this is crazy. But I'll call Caleb before dinner and we'll take it from there. All kidding aside, I can't fly that plane."

"If Caleb can't make it, I think you should sneak out the basement window tonight after everyone is asleep and go over to the Buckleys and check out the plane. I'll give you directions later," she said.

"You've lost your mind," I said.

She smiled up at me, reached out, and lightly touched my arm and put her arm around my waist. We were standing only inches apart.

"Let's go downstairs and deal with dinner," she said.

CHAPTER SIX

"You know you're in love when you can't fall asleep because reality is finally better than your dreams."

—Dr. Seuss

Jacob and Ruth were waiting at the bottom of the steps. I wondered if they had overheard our conversation then decided they hadn't, based on the looks on their faces.

"How is she?" Ruth said.

"Asleep. You guys were right. She needs to get out of here. Jacob, thanks again for making the call to Caleb." India paused, looked around, and then looked out the window. The light was still on and she saw her father still working in the shop.

"At dinner, I'm going to ask Dad to help us get her out of here tomorrow and explain why that needs to happen. I won't push it too far because if he says no, then we need a plan to get her out without his help, and by that, I mean behind his back. So if he starts really resisting and getting mad, I'll act like I'm agreeing to give it a few more days. Eli's going to call Caleb while we're cooking dinner to see if he can get a plane or helicopter in here or to the Buckleys' runway tomorrow. If he can't, then we're going to take the Buckleys' plane – Eli can fly us out.

"I know that that may sound crazy but it's our only option if we want to get Mom to a hospital quickly. To do that, we'll need a diversion to keep Dad busy while we get Mom out of bed, down the stairs, onto one of the ATVs and across to the Buckleys'. So Jacob, that will be your job. We'll have to keep him far way from here and busy. I'm saying all this now because we don't have much time and it's going to be harder for us to be together when he comes in from the shop. I realize this is a lot to process."

"I already have it," Jacob said. "Last week we started building the footings for a dock over on the feeder creek. He said he wanted to get it done this week and we haven't started yet. He was waiting for me to finish some log work down by the runway and I finished that today. The weather might still be bad tomorrow but weather never stops him from doing anything. It's a perfect plan. When we get over there and start building the dock, I'll tell him I need to run back to the shop. I'll intentionally leave something behind, then when I get to the shop I'll take the other ATV and join you and we'll get Mom to the Buckleys. Eli, how long have you been a pilot? Can you fly in low ceilings?"

"He's been a pilot for a while but he hasn't flown much the last few years," India interjected. "The conditions aren't ideal, so we'll all need to help."

"All need to help?" I mouthed silently to her behind Jacob and Ruth's backs. She smiled.

"One more thing," India said. "Eli's going to sneak out tonight and go over to the Buckleys' house to check out their plane. We don't want to get all the way over there with Mom tomorrow and have it be gone or out of commission somehow."

"Okay," said Jacob slowly. "I can go with Eli now when he calls Caleb, under the guise of showing him the property. Then while we're out I'll show him the path that leads to the Buckleys'. We also need a gun and a headlight for him if he's going over in the middle of the night. I'll bring both and leave them by the trail where you can find them when you get out tonight, Eli. And just for the record," he turned back to India and gave her a long look, "I think all of this sounds nothing short of crazy. Bat-shit crazy."

"Maybe," I agreed. Then another thought came to me. "We need to construct some type of stretcher or sling so we can get your mom onto the ATV. Maybe an old hammock or tent or anything else you have lying around that will hold her. We can lash the fabric to some two by fours. This is the most important part of our task—keeping her comfortable and safe while we move her. We also need to tell her what we're doing but not until a time when she's lucid, so she won't forget and accidentally tell your dad."

"I can get the hammock together," Ruth said. "Later tonight, when Dad's watching a movie, I'll slip down to the basement and find something that'll work. India, can you help me?"

"Of course."

"We're going to have to sedate your mom as much as possible," I said, thinking out loud. "I've seen people grind up extra-strength Tylenol into a paste and put it on the inside wrists of patients in pain. We can do that in combination with her pills."

"We've still got some prescription-strength Tylenol left over from my dad's injury," India said. "I can grind it up tonight into a powder. We can double up her pain meds before we move her tomorrow and I'll put the paste on her wrists and wrap them up. That's the best we can do.

"So," she added, "everyone be normal when Dad comes in and we'll just go about our business. Then we'll execute the plan according to what we just discussed. Eli, here's the SAT phone in case your cell doesn't work when you call Caleb."

As soon as she handed me the phone, the back door opened and her dad came into the mud room, just off the kitchen where we were all standing. We all exchanged worried looks, then quickly split up: India and Ruth went to the cupboards and began moving pots and pans around in the kitchen, I went to the living room to hide the phone, and Jacob headed down to the basement, maybe to get the gun and a headlamp.

"What's for dinner?" their father bellowed.

"Moose burgers with mashed potatoes and sweet peas," India said.

"Don't forget the beer. Where's Jacob and your friend?" he said, stepping into the kitchen.

"Jacob's in the basement and Eli's getting ready to go out. Jacob's going to show him the property and the feeder creek where the trout holes are. Maybe they'll throw in a line," India said.

"What are you talking about? It's pouring rain and gusting to thirty miles per hour. No way anyone can fish in that. I'm going upstairs to see your mother. I doubt she can come down yet, so let's fix her a tray." He walked through the kitchen and over to the staircase.

I listened to his heavy, plodding footsteps going up the steps, then I circled back into the kitchen, nodding first to India and then to Ruth as I walked past them to the mud room. Jacob quickly joined me and we put on our boots and heavy rain gear. Once we were ready I looked around the corner into the kitchen, where dinner preparation was underway.

"Okay. We're off. See you later." They both looked at me and nodded.

It was a pouring outside. Jacob and I exited through the back door and stayed close to the house as we circled it and headed out toward the river in front of the house. It was furiously windy, wet and cold. There were massive black rolling storm clouds over to the west and the temperature was quickly dropping. I figured it must have been in the low 40s, but with the wind chill it felt like the 20s. It was something between a once-in-a-century rain storm and an early winter snow storm, neither of which was good for our plan. The wind whipped us as the rain pelted down, pulling our raincoats in different directions. It also seemed close to hail or at least freezing rain.

"You barely know how to fly, do you?" Jacob yelled over the weather.

I looked over at him. He was taller and bigger than I was, but so young in so many ways. I considered how to respond.

"I'm qualified to fly the plane, Jacob. Under normal circumstances I wouldn't because of the weather and the fact that I haven't flown in a while. But I wouldn't do it if I didn't know I could get us there. Don't worry, we'll pull this off if we have to."

We trudged across the lawn, our boots sinking into the soft soil as we walked, water splashing up with each footfall. Water was everywhere. That's the thing with Alaska, when bad weather moves in, you better be prepared because it can get out of hand quickly and it can stay forever.

When we reached the edge of the lawn down by the river I looked back at the house. The master bedroom was in the rear, facing us, and I was hoping their dad wouldn't see me talking on the phone. I told Jacob to walk slower so I could make the call. There was so much wind and rain I doubted anyone could tell what we were doing anyway. I tried my cell phone first, holding it close to my face so my hood obscured it from view. There was no service, just as I'd suspected. I quickly got out the SAT phone and punched in Caleb's number on the keypad.

"Caleb," he said.

"Caleb. It's Eli and we have problems over here. We need to evacuate Helen tomorrow one way or another. She has a badly broken shoulder and we're convinced she had a stroke too."

"Okay," Caleb replied.

"The family's going to talk to their dad tonight and try to convince him to let us get her out of here. When India first broached the subject to him, he said absolutely no way she leaves. If he sticks to that we'll need your help. In fact, either way we'll need your help. If he agrees, we'll need you and if he doesn't we'll still need you, but it will be under different and difficult conditions."

The line went quiet.

"I'm not sure you know what you're getting into with option 2," Caleb said. "I can't off the top of my head envision a scenario where I land a plane on their landing strip and Dan is unaware of that happening, while you run the quarter mile from the house carrying a woman in a stretcher. Just don't see that working. Assuming I could land a plane in this weather."

"You wouldn't be flying in here in either situation. I assume you know the Buckleys' place next door. They have a grass runway which would help you land in this, and Dan wouldn't be alarmed by a plane flying in there. The difficult part is getting Helen over there and onto a plane without being noticed, not to mention how hard it will be to get her there in her condition."

"If we could make this happen, and that's a big if," Caleb said, "what do you think will happen when Dan calls one of his friends to come get him after we're airborne and he flies into Anchorage a half hour after we arrive and gets to the hospital and throws a monster shit fit? What's going to happen then? And I know this might not seem that important under the circumstances, but I'm a little worried about what's going to happen with my relationship with him. I'm a co-conspirator here and he would never forgive me. India has worked for me since she was old enough to walk and same for Jacob. I'm close to that family and I don't feel good about what this would do to my relationship with them as well as my relationship with the whole bush community around here. We trust each other. Our survival is built on trust."

"India told me how important you've been to them. But that's why you're their only option. I think that's why they look at you as the only person they can turn to. You are the one person who can save their mom."

"All right. Let's say I do this. The biggest concern is the massive front moving in from the west. Honestly, I haven't seen a storm this big in years, if ever, and it's barreling down on us. There are already airmen advisories all over Alaska including those for larger jets into Anchorage. With luck, I might be able to take off from here, but the likelihood of landing at the Buckleys' is remote. And if I can't land, I'll have to turn around and try to get back here. But who knows if that will be possible either—and then I'm screwed. I think the best option now is for you to call me after dinner and I'll listen to more weather forecasts in the meantime. I'll keep the SAT phone close by and we can talk more then."

"Fair enough," I said.

"And Eli. I told you before you left to watch yourself. It doesn't seem like you're doing a good job of that."

"I know."

Jacob was standing not far away next to the side of the house, easily within hearing distance of my side of the conversation with Caleb. When I disconnected the line he looked at me with a strained expression. We were getting deeper and deeper into a situation that seemed to have no good ending. And the rain seemed to be picking up if that was possible.

"What'd he say?" Jacob asked.

"That the odds are against us with the weather. The storm moving in is massive, and he doesn't think he can get here. But I think he'll try if we don't have any other alternatives and if there's at least a chance he can make it. I'm going to talk to him again after dinner."

Jacob continued to stand beside the house, giving me a look that wasn't hard to interpret. Rain was pouring off our hoods. We needed to get going but he just kept standing still, as if unable or unwilling to move. I saw a bolt of lightning over his shoulder and slowly counted the seconds to the thunder. One, two, three, four, five, then the boom. The storm was roughly a mile away and closing. Time was running out. If I was going to make it over to the Buckleys' later tonight to check out that plane, we had to leave now to look at the trail. I was still hoping we wouldn't need that plane, but if we did, we needed to know beforehand it was there and ready to fly.

"Jacob, show me the trail. We can drop the gun and headlamp at the trailhead and get back in time for dinner. We need to get out of this storm before it gets worse and before your dad gets wise to anything."

"This way," Jacob finally said.

I followed him to a spot where the forest was farthest away from the house, probably 100 yards from where we were. The trees there were particularly dense—short, prickly pines and alders. The rain was torrential now and I was soaked through despite my rain gear. Water poured off my hood and jacket and streamed down my legs like a creek overflowing its bank. It was also getting much colder. I didn't think there was any way Caleb would get in or I would get out under the present circumstances but I figured we might as well follow the plan for now.

Jacob was walking fast a few feet in front of me, both of us fighting the wind and rain. It was getting harder to walk across the saturated lawn and I couldn't hear anything above the noise of the wind. It was raining sideways and gusting to what must have been 40 mph or more. The wind was making a strange, mournful howl that I hadn't heard before.

When we approached the tree line Jacob stopped and looked back at me and then at the house, then motioned me forward. I could see a slight clearing ahead which I assumed was the trail. We walked into the tree line. The forest canopy provided a small respite from the elements. We pushed our hoods back, and I looked at Jacob. His face was completely soaked. It was monsoonal.

"Okay. This is the start of it. The trail is never used so I'm sure there are trees down and tons of obstructions, but for the most part it looks like this. Can you see it?" It was getting dark, and Jacob turned on the headlamp so we could see a few yards in front of us.

"Yeah, I see it," I said. "Let's go down the trail just a bit so I can see what it looks like away from the edge."

We walked thirty yards down the wide trail. It looked like it hadn't been used in years. There were faint tracks where an ATV or other small vehicle had left an imprint some time ago, but it was mostly overgrown with thick alders and weeds and all manner of brush on the path. I was worried about what I would encounter when I came back tonight. It wasn't quite nightfall yet, but I already couldn't see more than three feet in front of me. I had no idea how I was going to get to the Buckleys' and back in the middle of the night after India's father went to bed. And to top it off, I had no clear idea where I was going.

"When was the last time anyone used this trail?" I asked.

"I would say it's probably been three to four years since any of us has been over there."

"You said it's roughly four miles?"

"Give or take. In an ATV, I used to make it over in an hour or so. But there's a large ravine about halfway across and it can wash out if the river's running high. You'll need to be careful when you cross it. I can almost guarantee it will be flooded tonight."

"How flooded?"

"Completely." If you stay to the high side of the trail you'll see the ravine and the water as you approach. Also, keep scanning your headlight above, ahead, and to the sides of the trail. There could be bears moving around. You're probably not going to have an interaction with a bear and I don't want to scare you, but better be alert to it than not."

I looked over at him and smiled. "I'm a freaking office worker for Christ's sake. What the hell am I doing here?"

For the first time he laughed a deep hearty laugh. Relief. He smiled and put his hand on my shoulder. "Dude, if you hadn't been so interested in my sister you'd be sitting on Caleb's couch tending a fire and telling fish stories. Be careful what you wish for."

"For sure. Instead of that I'm going for a hike in the middle of a storm in the middle of the night to a place I've never been with bears scattered around to get to some abandoned place and check on a plane that may or may not be there. Oh, and then return and get back into the house without pissing off an angry father. Good luck with that."

We turned and walked back over to the edge of the forest. Jacob brought out a .357 handgun very similar to mine, put it and the headlight into a large sealable kitchen bag, and placed the bag carefully under a big pine bush a few feet inside the forest wall. He reached into his jacket pocket, brought out a piece of reflective tape, and tied to the top of the bush.

"You can't use the headlamp when you cross the lawn. Dad might see you, even though he sleeps pretty soundly. When we get back I'll give you an extra flashlight that you can turn on and off as you cross the lawn, just to keep your bearings. When you reach the edge of the forest, the flashlight beam will catch this reflective tape and you should be good to go."

"Got it," I said, not sure I had it.

"The gun's loaded and here are a few extra bullets," he said handing me the shells. "You good with a .357?"

"Yeah," I said. "I've got the same gun. Let's get back."

We turned, put our hoods back up, walked out into the clearing, and began the slog across the yard toward the house. We walked with our heads down, the rain and wind lashing at our backs while thunder and lightning filled the sky. I couldn't see much, so I stayed close to Jacob. I tried to visually mark where the trail was vis-à-vis the house and the direction I would head once I got out of the house tonight.

And I hoped upon hope the dad would see the obvious and help us get his wife to a hospital.

We rounded the edge of the house and headed for the back door. Everything was getting darker and the rain and wind were picking up. The jack pine trees lining the edge of the forest were bent double in the relentless straight-line wind. I had no idea how I was going to get out of the house later tonight, make it over to the trail and then to the Buckleys' house and back. And if the weather continued to deteriorate, the whole idea of getting India's mother out of here anytime soon was a pipe dream.

We walked up the steps to the backdoor and into the mud room. We were soaked and in no time the woven rug was completely wet. Jacob and I exchanged glances as we took off our gear. I shook out my jacket and hung it on a peg beside the dryer, above a floor vent which was throwing off heat. I hoped that it would dry out a bit before my adventure tonight. My jeans were soaked under my rain pants, and I needed to change them before dinner.

In the kitchen, India and Ruth were busy making dinner. It smelled delicious, and despite the situation, I was starving. We hadn't eaten since breakfast.

"I'm going downstairs to change my jeans. Be back in a second," I said.

I walked downstairs, pulled off my wet jeans, and hung them on a makeshift clothesline by my cot. The clothesline looked like it hadn't been used in years, but there was some furnace ductwork above it so the spot was warm and dry. I pulled on my only other pair of jeans and turned to go back upstairs. India was standing at the base of the stairs, wiping her hands on a dishrag. She had a sly smile on her face, a comment on my undress, but her eyes were serious.

"Hey," she said.

"Hey. What's going on?" I whispered going over to her.

"I'm worried about everything. I'm worried about dinner, I'm worried about you going to check out the Buckleys' place tonight, I'm worried about Caleb trying to get in here tomorrow. And of course I'm worried about you trying to fly us out if it comes to that."

"I know. Me too."

"We've got ourselves into a no-win position here. I'm really questioning what we're planning to do. But there aren't any alternatives that I can think of. Am I missing something? Is there some other plan I haven't thought of? Everything seems too risky, and there aren't any solid options I can be comfortable with."

"I know. I was just thinking the same thing," I said. "That there must be a better way out of this. Are you sure we couldn't do a boat? That seems like the least risky option to me - the only option that isn't completely weather dependent."

"The problem with a boat is that these rivers are really rough even in normal conditions. They're filled with swirling eddies, large boulder-strewn rapids that are impossible to navigate safely under normal conditions. Even if we weren't essentially in a flood at the moment, it would be a four-hour boat ride and rough the entire way. I don't see how we could keep Mom comfortable and safe for that long, especially given the weather. Those rivers are busting at their seams right now from one of the worst storms we've had in a long time and that can get really dangerous even if everyone's healthy. It would be worse than taking Mom on a roller-coaster now."

"Is there any possibility you could get a nurse or other medical professional to fly out here? Surely there are medical people who pay visits to the bush. What'd you do as a kid when someone got sick?"

"There are nurses who come out to the bush, like my Aunt Margie's friend, but they wouldn't come in this type of weather, and even if they could, I still think Dad would resist it. And frankly, I'm not sure any nurse could deal with a broken shoulder and a stroke."

"How sure are you that she had a stroke?" I asked.

"I'm almost certain. She doesn't have any idea what's going on around her and one side of her face seems like there's something wrong with it. I'm fairly sure she had at least a mild stroke."

We were standing close together at the bottom of the stairs. She looked up at me, and I could see she was exhausted from the stress.

"I can't believe this," she said.

"Me neither."

"I mean I can't believe I met you and we were having fun together and then I invite you into something that couldn't be farther from where we were and now we're embroiled in a mess. I'm sorry. I shouldn't have asked you to come. But now I need you."

"I know, and I'm happy to be here with you."

I looked down at her, my hair still wet. She reached up and softly wiped away a drop of water that was running down the side of my face, then gently brushed my hair back.

After a few moments she adjusted her shirt and turned and headed back upstairs. I followed.

CHAPTER SEVEN

"Now with God's help, I will become myself."

—Kierkegaard

"L et's eat," India yelled from the kitchen. "Ruth, go upstairs and tell Dad dinner's ready.

Jacob, India, and I seated ourselves at the dining room table. The table sat next to a sweeping picture window in the dining room, just off the kitchen. I sat next to India at the far end of the table, closest to the window and farthest away from where her dad would sit. Jacob was directly across from me. Ruth would sit next to him and their dad would be at the head of the table next to India.

Moments later we could hear talking and heavy footsteps on the stairs, and then Ruth and their dad came into the dining room. He looked unhappy. He pulled out his chair roughly and sat down, grabbed a burger from the tray and heaped his plate full of mashed potatoes and sweet peas. The rest of us passed the food around in silence.

"Dad, I know this is a bad time for you like it is for all of us with Mom being sick. But we want to talk to you about options to get her help," India said.

The father stopped eating and looked up at her with hard, wild, bloodshot eyes. He looked like he had been drinking. "I told you, no bastard doctors in Anchorage are going to do anything to your mother," he said, glowering at India. "We're not doing anything with Mom but keeping her here where we can attend to her."

"Let's just say she broke her shoulder. Wouldn't you want her to get help?" India responded.

"She didn't break her shoulder, for God's sake. She fell in the kitchen and grazed the end of the counter. She's had ten times the accidents of that and we never ran run off to Anchorage then."

"What if we fly a nurse in here. Aunt Margie's best friend is a field nurse. We could call Margie and see if she can get in touch with her friend and get her on a plane."

All eyes were on their dad. He'd stopped eating when the subject was broached. His face was turning red.

"I'm not sure what you and your boyfriend are doing here, but if you want to stay, you need to focus on getting your mother back on her feet. Period, end of story. Do you get that? And your boyfriend is leaving tomorrow. We have enough headaches around here."

"Fine. I just thought we should talk it through one more time. We'll focus on getting her better here. But Eli isn't leaving until I do."

I was trying to be as still as possible but I couldn't help looking down the table. He made a huff and went back to eating.

Dinner was quick after that. He ate and then pushed his chair back without a word, grabbed a beer from the fridge, and went back upstairs. We could hear him clomping down the hall, opening the master bedroom door, and closing it behind him. Then we could hear the faint sound of someone talking.

"Does the SAT phone work in the basement?" I asked anyone who might know.

"Unfortunately, not. It needs a clear shot at a satellite, so you need to go outside," Jacob said.

"Okay. I'm going to go outside and make the second call to Caleb while your dad is still upstairs in your mom's room."

I got up from the table and walked directly through the kitchen to the mud room and put on my still soaked rain pants, jacket and boots. I put the hood up and grabbed the SAT phone that was sitting in its recharge cradle, then opened the door and walked outside.

It felt like the weather had gotten even worse. I needed to get this done and fast - as I walked, I was bent double into the wind. Outside, it had to be gusting over 60 miles an hour and the rain was nearly horizontal. Between the booming thunder and lightning, the sky howled and bruised clouds were moving sickeningly lower, licking closer and closer to the treetops. I quickly ran to the back of the shop and punched in Caleb's number.

He answered on the first ring.

"Caleb"

"It's me. Things are not better over here. Dan is pissed as hell that we're here and he isn't agreeable to taking her anywhere or allowing a nurse in here. What are the odds that you can get here tomorrow?"

"Impossible. The weather rolling off the Cook Inlet is getting worse and it's barreling our way. What time do you want to pull this off?"

"It would be ideal to do it around ten a.m. By that time, weather allowing, Jacob and Dan will be over working on the dock, or at least not in the house, and I think we'd have enough time to get Helen over to the Buckleys."

"Keep the phone handy and I'll call you promptly at nine a.m. That would be the time I would have to take off from here—just in case there's a miracle and the weather clears. But that seems very unlikely, so whatever your Plan B is, I would refine that tonight."

"I don't even want to tell you what Plan B is," I said.

"Good, because I don't want to know. Call you in the morning." The line clicked dead.

I walked into the mudroom and took off my newly drenched jacket and boots.

As unlikely as it seemed, I was going to the Buckleys tonight, so I needed to get ready. I put everything in a specific place in the mudroom so I could remember where it was without turning on a light. My jacket on the last hook before the door, my boots just to the side of the door, my rain pants on top of my boots.

I walked into the kitchen just as India was finishing doing the dishes. She set the towel down beside the sink and motioned me to the kitchen table.

"You want a beer or water or anything?" she asked.

"No, I'm fine."

"You don't look encouraged."

"I'm not. Caleb think's there's zero chance of him getting here, but he'll call me at nine a.m., just when he would be taking off, to let me know if it will work. From speaking with him and from being outside, I'm 100 percent confident he won't be landing here tomorrow. But just in case, we need to know the Buckleys airstrip is ready and we can get your mom over there. So, as planned, I'll prep the Buckleys' plane tonight and have it ready in the event that he can't get here and we need to take a chance."

"What chance?" India said, as if it wasn't her idea to begin with.

"That I can fly it, in whatever weather there is. Taking off will be easier than landing, so even if even Caleb can't land safely in this weather I should be able to get the plane into the air," *Who was I kidding*, I thought, even as I said the words. *Can I really do that? What was I getting myself into?* Still I continued planning out loud, projecting confidence. "Once I get us safely in the air I'll have to navigate successfully to Anchorage. I hope to God there's an Anchorage sectional map in that plane. I have no idea where Anchorage is from here and I'm not qualified to fly in instrument conditions—strictly visual flight—so I need a map or I need clear weather. And we won't be getting clear weather."

"Let's discuss this later. I want to go upstairs and see what's up with Mom and Dad. I want him to calm down so he goes to bed at his normal time and isn't focusing on what we're doing or suspecting anything. We need to make this work."

She turned and went upstairs and I heard her walk down the hall toward the master bedroom, then quietly open and close the door. After that I could only hear indistinct murmuring.

I went to the computer sitting on a desk in a corner of the living room, pushed the space bar, and the monitor blinked to life. I sat down and clicked the Google icon. The internet connection was live, and I Googled "how to fly a Cessna 172." It had been several years since I had flown and then always with an instructor beside me.

As usual, there were thousands of videos from which to choose. I selected "takeoff, pattern and landing" and watched a two-minute YouTube primer—it all looked familiar. Jacob and Ruth came into the room, and I checked my email then clicked off. I didn't want them seeing my browser open to this topic. As I stood up India rounded the bend from the staircase and came over to me.

"How is she?" I asked.

"She's awake now. But it's clearer than ever that she had a stroke. The left side of her face appears slack and she comes in and out of awareness. She's disoriented and doesn't seem to know where she is. At this point I think the shoulder is almost secondary. She's not in much pain because of the meds we're giving her. We need to move forward with the plan—she needs to get out of here. And that means you have to find your way over to the Buckleys' house tonight. I'm sorry to send you out this in horrible weather. Maybe we should let Jacob go?"

"No," I said, sounding more resolute than I felt. "Jacob doesn't know anything about the plane so I have to be the one to check it out. What time will your dad go to bed? It's about seven-thirty now."

"He's essentially in bed now. But he'll get up once more to use the bathroom and brush his teeth, then he'll get back in bed with her and sleep all night. Or at least I hope he will."

"So by nine tonight he'll be down for the count."

India nodded.

"I'm going to lay out my clothes for tonight and get ready. Come down when you're finished with whatever you have to do now, and we can talk before I leave."

"Ok."

I headed down to the basement. Jacob was standing by a workbench that ran the length of the east side of the basement. The work bench light was on and tools were out.

"Hey. What's up?"

"Nothing and everything," he said nervously. "I'm trying to think about how we should build the sling for Mom."

"Do you have what you need?"

"I think so." I moved over to my bed and rummaged through my backpack for some warmer clothes. I pulled out the heavy fleece shirt I'd brought and my long underwear. I sat on the bed and replaced my socks with a thicker version with thinsulate insulation. My rubber boots weren't insulated and it was getting colder.

"What are the odds are of us getting out of here tomorrow?" he asked.

"I'd say the best case is maybe 20 percent, depending entirely on the weather at this point. That's the only thing holding us up. If the weather breaks or slows down, I think we have a shot, assuming you can keep your dad over at the dock."

"That won't be a problem. He told me tonight we had to get to work early tomorrow so I know he's focused on getting that dock started."

"Are the keys to the ATV in the ignition?" I asked.

"Yeah, and earlier today I went out and made sure it's full of gas. Tomorrow morning Dad will drive the truck over to the dock and I'll take the red ATV. The black one is the one you'll take. Runs like a charm so you won't have any problems."

He glanced toward the stairs. "I'm waiting for Ruth to get down here so we can build the sling for Mom."

"How's it going to work?"

"We're going to make it out of an old hammock. I'll weld four, four-foot metal poles to create a frame. We'll use the old hammock to make a sling, and tonight when Dad's sleeping I'll go into the shop and weld the frame to passenger side of the ATV. When you get Mom ready, all you'll have to do is insert the sling onto the frame. I'm also going to leave a small trailer by your ATV because the sling will take up all the room on the ATV. Ruth and India will need to ride in the cart."

"It sounds like a plan."

"What sounds like a plan?" India peered under the railing. She came down the stairs and over to where we were standing.

"Jacob was just telling me how the sling will work. It's genius," I said.

"Good."

She looked from one of us to the other. Jacob held her gaze for a moment, then turned back to the work bench. "I need to get going on this," he said.

India and I went over to my sleeping area and sat on the edge of the bed. "I'm going to bed fairly soon because I want the second floor of the house to calm down early tonight. Ruth will as well, and Jacob can finish the sling. What time are you going?" she asked.

"It's all based on what time your dad will be sleeping, but assuming he's out by ten, I'll leave right after that. I figure the earlier I get out of here the earlier I'll get back. Then I can catch a little sleep before we leave tomorrow."

"Are you good with the route over there?"

"No. But I'll make it happen."

She smiled an exhausted smile. Her hair was disheveled, falling around her face. She leaned in close to me, her shoulder edging its way under my arm, as if getting closer and warmer would somehow make the cold reality of the situation go away. I put my arm around her. She rested her head on my chest and I could hear her breathing. I realized she was falling asleep. Still sitting up beside me.

"Hey, I think it's time for bed," I said.

She stirred and looked up at me, then unwrapped herself. "I'm bone tired."

"I'm sure. You want me to walk you upstairs?"

"No. You stay here and get ready. And see if you can take a nap before you leave. I'm worried about you too."

"No need to worry," I said, trying to look braver than I felt. I'll be fine. I should be back here by twelve-thirty or one. Then I'll sleep and be ready to go by morning."

We walked over to the staircase. Jacob was quietly working on the sling in the other part of the basement. At the edge of the stairs India stopped and turned to me. "I'll be thinking of you tonight, sending you good thoughts. Come back safely and be careful."

She touched the side of my face and turned to go up the stairs.

I walked back over to the bed and lay down. I set my watch for 9:45 p.m. I had an hour and a half before I needed to leave. I laid my head on the pillow and was immediately asleep.

I got up and got dressed at 9:45. The furnace was on and heat was rolling out of the vents in the basement. I walked up the darkened steps to the kitchen, carefully tiptoeing in my socks so as not to disturb anyone or anything. I got to the kitchen landing and turned left toward the mud room. The beam of a small flashlight appeared in the corner of the mudroom, scaring me out of my sleepy haze. Then I saw that India was standing there, completely dressed in her rain gear and ready to go. She put her finger over her lips signaling me to be quiet.

I put on my gear and we carefully opened the back door. We stepped outside and were immediately hit by 60 mile an hour flat-line winds. The rain was still coming in sheets and the wind was making a horrendous howl as it flew across the tundra and hit the house and outbuildings. A metal clanging was coming from the area of the shop, probably some metal roofing that got dislodged. I reached for India and she grabbed my hand, then my arm, and we started walking across the lawn, bent double, the wind whipping at our jackets, the water halfway up our calves. Midway across the lawn I stopped and looked back at the house. Everything was still dark.

When we got close to the forest I briefly switched on the flashlight so I could see the trail opening. We walked into it, went fifteen feet into the forest, and stopped. It was suddenly quieter and somewhat drier. The wind and rain were diffused by the forest canopy. We pulled off our hoods and looked at one another.

"Are you freaking crazy?" I asked.

"Maybe, but I just couldn't stay in bed lying awake and have you find your way over to the Buckleys' alone. I made a decision. This will be better with the two of us going, I promise."

She was resolute, standing there looking at me with so many issues on her mind yet knowing I shouldn't go alone and deciding against all reasonable odds that she should go with me. I looked at her and saw strength and realized there was something about her that was different.

"Let's get the gun and headlight," I said.

I used the flashlight to find the small pile of brush at the edge of the trees where Jacob had left the reflective-tape marker. The headlamp and gun were still safely in place and dry. I put the gun in the front pocket of my jacket.

"Let me have the headlamp and I'll take the lead on the hike over," India said. "I've walked this trail dozens of times and it'll be easier for me to navigate if I'm in the front. You can take the flashlight and stay right behind me. I'll scan the trail and you scan the areas to our sides as we walk."

I handed her the headlamp and she fixed it on her head, then pulled up her hood. I shined the flashlight on the trail. It was like a ten-foot-wide forest hallway with thick, dense walls of trees and brush lining both sides. The trail floor was covered in four-inch-deep pine needles. I lifted the flashlight, looked farther down the trail, and saw nothing but a maze of fallen trees and limbs that littered the path, one obstruction after another. The trail got narrower at the end of the beam. I glanced at the backlit face of my watch – 10:20 pm. We started down the trail.

We were somewhat protected by the thick forest canopy, but the noise of the storm was still horrific above and around us. It sounded like the world was coming apart at its seams. The trees, many of them generations old, were creaking, groaning, and heaving from side to side. There was no moonlight because of the cloud cover and it was utterly dark. As we walked, I scanned the forest with my light and periodically saw eyes staring back at us from the trees. But no bears yet, just fox, marten and other eyes peering at us, all wondering who was disturbing their night. The earthy smell of dense forest filled the air, a combination of spruce and pine, water, and all manner of wildlife. It was rich and thick and foreboding. Cold and wet.

Fifty yards into our journey the trail made a sharp left turn. Before the bend a huge tangle of brush, tree limbs, and weeds was lying in a large pool of water in the middle of the trail. It looked like a tree had fallen and taken other trees with it and they were now overgrown with brush. As we approached the tangle I put my hand on India's arm to slow our approach. It wasn't hibernation time and and this spot was a perfect bear den, dense enough for protection and sheltered from the elements. I pulled out my gun and chambered a round. We kept walking, taking a wide route around the mess to give us about an arm's length between us and the side wall of the trail on one side and the tangle on the other. Whenever we looked to the side or scanned a certain area with our lights, the other parts of the forest instantly became ink black.

Fifty yards beyond the tangle and the left turn that came after it, we found ourselves standing at the edge of a steep decline, what must've been the drop off into the ravine Jacob had told me about. Even in the deep darkness, we could see that the trail led downward at maybe a 30-degree angle. I could hear water rushing at the bottom. We shined our lights below and saw that the entire trail was flooded at the bottom of the ravine, the water moving fast from left to right, away from the river. The ravine looked like it was about 50 feet deep from where we stood, its steep sides covered in heavy, dense brush. The water crossed our path and disappeared into the forest to the right. It was impossible to see the river in the darkness and we couldn't hear anything over the howling of the wind and the rushing of the water.

We started down the bank of the ravine toward the water.

"I assume this the flooded area Jacob was talking about?" I yelled above the storm.

India stopped and looked back at me, her headlamp blinding me. "Yeah. It's been years and years since I've seen it flood this badly. Once we get past this the trail levels out and we should be good."

"That looks deep," I said. "Can we walk around it?"

"The ravine begins to get shallower about 75 yards into the woods to the right, away from the river. Let's walk along the edge for a ways and see how impassable the forest is."

We turned to the right, walking directly into the dense forest. It looked impenetrable, a wall of thick brush and trees. The ground was muddy and there were devil's club bushes everywhere with their razor-sharp thorns. We bushwhacked through the undergrowth, branches and thorns scraping against our clothes, every step a challenge. The entire world seemed wet and cold and piercingly dark. I had no idea how we were going to get an ATV through here, let alone an ATV with a sick woman strapped to the top.

We made our way slowly through the thick morass one step at a time, losing sight of the ravine from time to time as we changed course slightly to avoid large downed trees or large clumps of bushes that blocked our way, listening to the water at the bottom of the ravine so as not to get lost. India was only five feet in front of me but I could barely see her through the thick undergrowth and unrelenting sheets of rain being thrown from the trees. The wind was ferocious and tree limbs fell around us nearly continually. Everywhere I looked there were downed trees that looked like perfect bear dens.

Twenty-five minutes later the bottom of the ravine began to rise slightly and I assumed that shortly it would end and we would be on level ground, then we could start our circle back to the trail. India was still ahead of me, walking carefully and continually looking back at me to ensure we were still close together. I had my gun out just in case we disturbed a bear.

Suddenly India stopped and held up her hand without looking back at me. I cautiously made my way to her. She pointed to an area about thirty yards ahead where the ravine appeared to end. "It looks like we can safely cross over there," she yelled. "I see water but it looks shallow."

She proceeded carefully and I followed her. When we got to where it appeared we could safely cross the ravine we went slowly down a small bank where the bottom was nearly dry. We scrambled up the other side and swung back to the east, the way we had come, now on the other side of the ravine. It took us twenty minutes to get back to the trail. Once we were there we stopped and India looked over at me and smiled. I was soaked inside my clothes from sweat even though the temperature was still dropping.

"Holy shit," I said, yelling over the noise of the wind. "That was way worse than I thought. I have no idea how we're going to get your mom through this. There's no way an ATV can make it through that underbrush."

"I know," India yelled. "I have no idea. Let's finish what we're doing. On the way back we can look around a bit and maybe find another spot away from the ravine that's closer to the trail. At the very least we can bring a machete when we come back with Mom, to cut our way through some of those problems."

I looked at my watch. It was now eleven. It had taken us nearly forty minutes to walk along just a small portion of the trail. I tapped her on the shoulder and showed her my watch. She said nothing.

She turned and found the trail again and we began walking. The sides of the forest appeared as walls once again, aiding us as we worked our way further into the forest on the other side of what I presumed to be the biggest obstacle. The trail at this point was narrower than before, the walls closing in tighter as we walked.

Native people believe that forests are alive, that they live and breathe and that when you move through them they watch and listen. I have felt the presence of Others many times over my many years of walking through the back country while fishing or hunting or hiking or climbing. Not humans or animals: Others. Tonight I hoped they were watching as our sentries, our protectors, helping us move us safely through our journey. This was as rough a patch of forest as I had ever seen.

Further along, the trail started gradually moving uphill and the tall pines we had come through were replaced by shorter trees and larger patches of alders. From time to time I could see over the tops of the trees and make out the intensity of the sky. Dark, menacing clouds slashed across it and occasionally there was a flash of lightning followed by a boom of thunder. The rain came in waves that splashed over us now that we were in less dense forest. I looked at my watch again. It was 11:45. We had been on the trail for nearly two hours.

Up ahead the trail veered sharply off to the right, then appeared to climb steeply. Beyond the turn I saw a rock outcropping that I couldn't see past. We kept hiking, India moving faster as we climbed up the trail. Finally we reached the rock outcropping and through the darkness I saw a broad meadow beyond. Sitting at the far edge of the forest was a house, several out buildings and a large hangar, unmistakable even in the dark. The Buckleys' at long last.

CHAPTER EIGHT

"*Every particular in nature, a leaf, a drop, a crystal, a moment in time is related to the whole, and partakes of the perfection of the whole.*"

—Ralph Waldo Emerson

We dashed across the expanse of lawn to the house, buffeted by howling winds and lashes of cold rain. India opened the door and we stumbled inside. The room was dark and cold. But it was warmer than outside, which led me to believe the heat had been left on. I found a light switch beside the door, flipped it on, and saw we were standing in a kitchen that clearly hadn't been used in some time. There were cobwebs along the back of the sink area and the refrigerator was open and dark.

"We made it," India said. "Thank God the Buckleys leave the door unlocked. We need to get warm." She said it wasn't unusual for Alaskans living in the bush to leave their doors unlocked when they weren't there, that it was considered good form to allow anyone who might be in trouble to use your place when you weren't around.

I looked at my watch. It was nearly midnight. It had taken us well over two and a half hours to make the crossing on foot. "That was something, coming over here," I said. "I can't imagine how we're going to get your mom here in an ATV. It seems inconceivable."

India looked at me silently and I could see that she agreed.

We were completely soaked despite our rain gear. Water was everywhere and was pooling on the hardwood floor near the rear entrance where we stood on a rug with 'welcome to our house' embroidered in the center of it. We shed our coats and took off our soaked pants, boots, and socks. I wrung our socks out in the kitchen sink. "By the way, did you get in touch with the Buckleys'?" I asked, standing at the sink. "Are they good with Caleb using the field and-or me using their airplane to get us out of here?"

"Uh, no. I didn't have time to call them. Besides, it would have been impossible with everything happening in the house. We're going to have to do this ourselves and ask for forgiveness instead of permission if we have to fly out of here."

"Okay," I said dubiously. "We're on a tight timeline, so let's head for the hangar and see what we're up against." I had a knot in my stomach that there was a chance I would actually have to do this.

"I'd like a second before we do that," she said, leaning with her back against the counter, facing me. We were exhausted and soaked. Her hair was a mess and she was still wearing the headlamp. At least it was turned off now. We were both muddy from our mid-thighs down. I stood there looking at her, waiting.

"It's strange, but all the way over here I wasn't thinking about what was in front of us in the next 24 hours, or the danger or the weather or the ravine or how we were going to get Mom out. I was thinking about how I've only known you four days and here you are risking everything for me. I can't tell you what that means. I want you to know how much I appreciate this. You're an amazing man."

My feet felt like they were anchored to the floor. I looked around the kitchen and for the first time understood the gravity of what we were doing.

"I've never done anything like this in my life—obviously," I said. "But we're doing the right thing. I don't really know any of you, but I'm proud to call you my friends. You're amazing people."

She walked over to me, pulled off her headlamp, and brushed her hair away from her face. She was so wet it looked like she had just gotten out of the shower. She put the headlamp on the counter and unzipped the light jacket she had on under her rain gear. Then she unzipped mine. She put her arms around my waist and pulled herself in to me. Nothing separated us but our underwear tops. She kissed me gently. Once, then again. And then she kissed me in a way that carried with it both the weight of our situation and the relief of sharing an honest moment. We stayed locked in each other's arms, kissing in the middle of a deserted house in the middle of nowhere, with only a tenuous plan for how to unentangle our situation and get out alive.

We turned on the generator sitting outside the back door, then the yard lights and any other lights we could find and stepped out of the house. There was no danger in anyone seeing us at this point and we needed to make the most of our time. We walked quickly across the lawn to the hangar, once again bent double in the rain and wind. The side hangar door was unlocked. I found a light switch inside next to the door and flipped it on. A series of lights clicked on in succession across the large pole building, illuminating the huge hangar, which held a boat and an ATV as well as a plane. In the middle of the hangar stood a 1960s-era Cessna 172, outfitted in true bush fashion. It had huge smooth tires and an oversized prop and had been retrofitted with new exhaust pipes that flared out from each side of the front cowling. Its metal side was full of dents and it was painted a deep black with yellow pinstripe detail running from front-to-back.

I walked around it, admiring the lines and appreciating the fact that someone had taken such meticulous care of its restoration and upkeep. I went over to the pilot's door, opened it, and got in. The key was in the ignition. It had the latest Garmin avionics package, not that that would do me much good with my experience, but it was nice to have as an interactive map—I could use it to track our progress toward Anchorage. The seats were lined with comfortable white memory foam wrapped in thick sheepskin.

India was standing in the middle of the hangar looking over at me and the plane, her arms across her chest. "Well?" she said.

"It's beautiful. Too bad it can't fly itself. Let me see if we have a battery."

I turned the key and the dashboard sprang to life. Within a few seconds all the gauges went live. It appeared someone had left this plane ready to fly. Everything looked perfect.

I turned the key to off and stepped out of the plane. "I'm going to do a safety check just in case we need to fly this." I opened the hood and checked the hoses and the oil. I looked for anything amiss, any belts that were worn, any evidence of mice eating fuel lines. Everything looked in showroom condition. Next I checked the wings, the flaps, the tail, the ailerons and the tires—all in working condition if not better. Last, after I had closed everything up, I went back into the plane, turned the key to on again, and checked the fuel levels—both tanks were full. I also found a central/south central Alaska sectional map that showed the air routes in and around Anchorage. I put that in the pocket of my jacket. If this plane needed to fly, it appeared as though it could.

"Let's check the hangar door," I said, moving over to a touchpad located just to the right of the huge hangar door directly in front of the plane. Luckily the touch-pad didn't require a code. I pressed both buttons. The second one kicked the lift into action and the door opened. As it rose, wind from the outside blew in, bringing with it a fusillade of leaves and twigs and rain, and we were instantly reminded that the real obstacle to success here was not this plane or Caleb or India's dad or even my questionable ability to fly, but the weather itself. Before the door opened completely I hit the button again and the door began to reverse and close.

I looked over at India, still standing in the middle of the hangar bay. "We're good with this airplane. It can do whatever we require of it, assuming I can remember how to fly. Now we need to figure out how we're going to get your mom here without killing her and how we're going to fly in this weather without killing us all. Let's think about this."

India walked over to me and took off her jacket and I did the same. It was warm and comfortable inside the hangar. The Buckleys had left the radiant heat working in the hangar, presumably to keep the plane's avionic systems in good shape over the winter. It was 12:45 in the morning—way later than I had planned. We were living on borrowed time. I slid the pilot seat forward and climbed into the back. She followed

89

me on the passenger side and we started arranging a makeshift bed in the back for her mom. We were able to get the rear seats to recline forward and lay flat, which gave us what I figured to be six or more feet of flat space that could double as a bed.

"I think once we get her in here, she'll be fine," I said. "You can ride up front with me, and Ruth and Jacob can sit beside her. The problem is going to be getting her in here comfortably and safely. I'm also a bit concerned about weight and balance. With all of us in here, that'll be five people, which would max out what this plane can handle, not even counting the weight of fuel. In fact, I think we'll be over the edge of safety. You never want to fly in bad conditions being heavy." I looked over at her. "Honestly, now that I think about it, one of us needs to stay behind."

India nodded as if she had already thought of that. "I think it should be Jacob," she said. "He can just keep working with Dad until they decide to break and then either act like he wasn't aware we were leaving when Dad finds out, or just take Dad's wrath and deal with it."

"Except we'll need him going on the trail and getting her into the plane. If anything happens on the way over we'll need his help. In fact, I don't think we'd be safe making that crossing without him, given the water level in the ravine and the bushwhack we might have to make around the ravine. What about leaving Ruth behind? She's the youngest and the least likely to help in the crossing."

"Also, the least able to stand up to Dad and the lightest from a weight and balance standpoint," she said, looking at her hands for a moment, then appearing to make a decision. "Okay. Let's plan on leaving Ruth behind. I can talk to her in the morning."

I used some blankets stowed in the far rear of the airplane and to make a make-shift bed. We took the headrests from the rear seats and created walls lining both sides of the bed to help hold India's mother in place. We found a small dog bed under the front seat and cut it open to use as a pillow. When we were finished India climbed out of the plane and I looked around the interior to ensure everything was in place. It looked adequate, if not exactly cozy.

The wind whipped us when we stepped out of the hangar and back into the night. We decided to leave all of the exterior lights on to help us check the condition of the runway. We struggled across the expanse of lawn, once again bent nearly double against the wind, using a high-beam aeronautical flashlight we'd found in the hangar to illuminate the landscape in front of us. Sweeping the beam back and forth, we eventually located a section of grass at the end of what appeared to be a taxiway that looked like the runway. It was thirty feet wide and clearly differentiated in grass height from everything around it.

"Let's try to find the end of it and remember its location in relation to the hangar," I screamed over the howl of the wind. We found the south end of the runway and walked the 2000-yard length of the strip checking for low spots, water, or other obstructions that could impede either Caleb's arrival or our departure. We spent at least 45 minutes clearing limbs, brush, and one large tree from the runway, the wind tearing at our jackets and keeping us off balance. Luckily there were no water hazards, but we would need to do the same thing again tomorrow before anyone flew in or out.

"Let's get the hell out of here," India yelled at me. She motioned toward the house a hundred yards away, now bathed in the glow of its outside lights.

We ran to the house and leaned against the outside wall. "Jesus Christ!" India shouted.

"Unreal!" I yelled back. The weather had transitioned from rain and wind to straight-line wind. Impossible for flying.

I showed her my watch again. It was 1:30 a.m. She shook her head. We had to get back to her house before her dad got up or he'd know we were up to something and all hell would break loose.

"Let's go inside," I yelled.

We huddled together and moved toward the door, heads down, backs bent. We walked into the kitchen exhausted and not so much wet as battered by the winds. In the kitchen we took off our jackets, hats, rain pants, and boots in silence and stood looking at each other, still panting, both of us now in our wet long underwear.

"That's incredible," I said.

"Yeah. I know we should hurry back, but I need a break before we start. I'm beat."

"Me too. Let's get warm."

We went into the living room. There were two long sectional sofas and two large club chairs configured in a semi-circle around a split stone-fireplace of impressive size, maybe ten feet across and ten feet high where it disappeared into the ceiling. She walked around the living room, turning on a couple of table lamps. I walked to the fireplace and shone my light up into the flue. It was closed, and I grabbed the handle and opened it. A crescendo of leaves and pine needles fell onto the hearth and a burst of cold wind came through the opening. Beside the fireplace was a neatly stacked pile of split wood. I turned to India and motioned to the fireplace. She nodded, and I walked into the kitchen and opened drawers until I found a box of matches. Then I returned and placed some small kindling on the dry leaves and pine needles that had fallen down when I opened the flue, then added some small split logs. I leaned into the hearth, struck a match, and ignited the leaves and needles. A fire soon began licking at the sides of the larger sticks, then the logs.

I heard a movement and looked over my shoulder. India was standing by a large armoire in the corner, holding up a bottle of whiskey and two small glasses, looking at me with a sly smile.

"You can't be serious," I said.

"We can take a break. Nobody will be up at the house until at least seven, and it will only take us two hours to get back. If we went back now we wouldn't sleep anyway. Let's get warm and have a drink and relax. This is the first time we've had a chance to just take a moment in days, and I'm tired and I want a drink."

The fire was roaring behind me now, casting shadows in the darkness at the edges of the room. The living room was constructed in a semi-circle and there were windows along the entire expanse of the outside curved wall, which probably faced the river but I didn't know for sure because it was dark. The windows shook as the wind howled out of the north. The fire began to gradually warm the room, its heavenly tentacles reaching my damp arms and legs as I sat on the hearth. I went over to the largest couch located directly in front of the fireplace and picked up a heavy Hudson Bay wool blanket and held it up to India. She carried the whiskey and glasses and slipped onto the couch and I placed the blanket on top of her. I helped her sink into the comfort of the couch. The glow from the fireplace illuminated her face.

CHAPTER NINE

"I sat there and forgot and forgot, until what remained was the river that went by and I who watched... Eventually the watcher joined the river, and there was only one of us. I believe it was the river."

—Norman Maclean

S he rested against the arm of the sofa, a couple of pillows tucked behind her. She'd found a towel in the bathroom and had wrapped her long hair up in it. She'd also put on a pair of old sweatpants that she'd found somewhere. I sat in the middle of the couch and pulled the blanket over both of us. The fire roared, sending heat across the room. She poured each of us a small glass of whiskey and we toasted. It was just the right medicine.

"You know what I was just thinking?" I offered.

"I have no idea, but please make it uplifting. I'm in the mood for some good news."

"I'm supposed to leave for New York the day after tomorrow. Sorry about it not being uplifting but's it the truth. Think about what we were doing when we were fishing—the utter beauty of every moment—and look where we are now. And I'm supposed to get on a plane in two days and fly back to New York as if my vacation was over." I put air quotes around the word vacation.

I paused and looked at her. "I'm just curious: What happens next in my life? Where do I go from here? I almost can't imagine resuming my old life after what we've been through the past few days."

"I said uplifting. You're not being uplifting," she said.

"I know. But it's the truth and it's reality."

I got up, walked over to the fire, adjusted the burning logs, and added several more to the fire. It was roaring and the room was finally, fully warm. My long underwear was starting to dry. I went into the kitchen and turned off the light, then turned off all but one light in the living room, a small lamp on the end table next to her. I found four candles in the armoire, placed them around the room, and lit them. I sat back down on the sofa, covered up again with the heavy blanket, and looked over at her. She was watching the fire, her hair dry and the towel on the floor next to her. The room was bathed in the soft glow of candlelight and the fire cast shadows across the room. Her hair fell in long circles around her face so I could only see her nose and eyes. In the quiet darkness of the room, I noticed the deep tan of her skin and the cross around her neck. She appeared to be someplace else now, deep in thought, the half-empty whiskey glass held loosely in her hand. Finally, she looked over at me and smiled a loose, relaxed smile.

"Who could have imagined this?" she asked.

"Not me. Not in a million years."

I was awakened by the sensation of warmth on my cheek, and when I opened my eyes I was in a sunlit room. India was sound asleep, her head resting on a pillow. I was lying partly on top of her, my head resting on a pillow on her hip, my legs extending along the outside edge of the long couch. I looked at my watch, it was 6:30 a.m. We had fallen into a deep sleep that had lasted for hours and were in trouble. We had badly overslept on the day when everything had to happen in a very short, precise window. At the same time, our sleep had been deep and good and probably what we needed. I looked around the room. The fire had long gone out, the light was off, the candles were extinguished, and most of the whiskey was gone from the bottle. I couldn't remember when we had fallen asleep, but we couldn't have slept for more than a few hours.

I sat up, still wearing my long underwear. India stirred and I gently rubbed her leg. After a brief moment her eyes fluttered open and she smiled at me sleepily. Then a look of panic overtook her and she sat bolt upright.

"Oh my God, we slept all night. Shit! What're we going to do!"

"It's okay, I have an idea."

She looked at me silently.

"Look, we're late. We screwed up. We overslept, which on one hand is bad but on the other hand not so bad. We needed sleep. The weather still sucks so we'll never get your mom out today anyway. Let's just take it easy, have some coffee, assuming we can find some, then hike back to your house. We'll tell everyone we got up really early and went for a walk checking out the damage from the storm, and nobody will be the wiser. Jacob and Ruth may be a bit freaked out by us not being there, but they'll have no option but to wait until we return. We'll leave one day later, and maybe this weather will have blown out by then and Caleb will be able to fly in. At least it can't get worse. It already looks like it might be improving since the sun's out"—I looked through the window—"although there are some mean clouds off to the west. Sound okay?"

She lay back down in her nest and snuggled the blanket around her. "Keep me warm," she said.

I got up and walked over to the fireplace. Some embers still remained. I put some kindling in, blew into the embers, and watched them turn pale red, then bright red as they were encouraged back to life. I kept blowing and a small flame appeared and the bottom of the kindling pile caught fire. In a few minutes we had a solid fire. I placed some smaller logs, then two larger logs on top. This should be good for some time.

"That's not what I meant by keeping me warm," she said from the couch. I turned around. She was holding the blanket up, showing me the spot where she wanted me to lie beside her.

"Give me two more minutes. I can't function well without coffee. Let me get it going before I get back into that nest." In the kitchen I quickly found the coffee in a cupboard above the coffee maker, got the pot brewing, then returned to the living room. The fire was blazing and warmth was once again creeping through the room toward the couch. The windows were shaking with the wind and the early-morning sunlit sky was now a deep overcast. It looked like it could rain anytime. India raised the blanket again as I approached the sofa. I lay down in front of her and she spooned me from behind. We watched the fire and listened to the wind blow. The aroma of fresh coffee soon made its way into the living room. I rolled over so I was face to face with her. Her green eyes were flecked with gold. I brushed a few loose strands of her hair behind her ear so I could see her face. Our noses were nearly touching.

I drew back, then kissed her long and deeply. I could smell the musky scent of our night in the deep woods wafting up between us. We smelled like pine and water and aspen. I slipped my hands under her loose shirt. Her breasts were silky smooth and firm. She threw her leg over mine and moved in closer as her nipples hardened.

We were intertwined as tightly as two people can be, both seeking more of the newness of the other. There was an immediacy to our passion, whether that was because we had to move forward with our day and our plan and that was all too much to consider or because this might be both our beginning and our end. I didn't know which, but in an instant our clothes were off and everything that we had been holding back over the past few days poured fourth in a potpourri of scattered clothes and intertwined arms and legs. Finally, she was on top and I encouraged her as she moved faster and deeper, both of us ending in eruptions of passion that at least I had never experienced before. Finally, we lay on the couch, soaked in sweat and holding each other so tightly I thought I might never let her go.

"I hope you like black coffee," I called to her from the kitchen once we had settled from our love making. "The only thing I can offer is sugar or some powdered milk I found in the pantry."

"Milk and sugar please." It was now a few minutes after seven and we needed to start heading for home. I looked into the living room from the kitchen. She was sitting up on the couch watching the fire, wrapped in the heavy wool blanket.

"I have to go to the bathroom – be right back," she said. She walked down the hallway between the kitchen and the living room, smiling at me as she went through the kitchen, her breasts exposed as she pulled her tee shirt on. Her sweatpants hung low on her hips and her stomach and the top of her butt were exposed. I made our coffees and went back into the living room to wait, stoking the fire for the last time before we left.

"That smells fantastic," she said when she came back, pointing to our steaming mugs resting on the coffee table.

"It tastes even better."

She sat close beside me on the couch. As we drank our coffee we stared out the window at the river, pitching and frothing as it raced past the house, 150 yards away. We had come in from the west, walking parallel to the river. It was clear now that the ravine would continue to be flooded given the ferocity of the river.

"Our story for Dad is that we both woke up early and took a long hike along the river. We couldn't sleep so we went out to check for any damage around the property. It had stopped raining by then and we left the house around six and ended up walking for a few hours. I figure if we leave at seven-thirty, in a half hour, we should be back home around nine-thirty because it won't take us as long with daylight. Dad and Jacob will be long gone. We'll check on Ruth and Mom and then head over to the dock and see what the men are up to."

"Do you really think they'll be out working in this weather?" I said.

"Oh yeah, nothing stops Dad from working outside. He goes nuts hanging around the house during the day. Plus it's stopped raining, at least for now. It looks like it's calmed down quite a bit out there."

"Okay. We need to figure out how to cross the water in the ravine so we can get the ATV across. And when we get back to your house we need to check the weather, call Caleb, and somehow talk to Ruth and Jacob—all in addition to dealing with your dad. So we're leaving here in thirty minutes?"

"Yes, even though I don't want to," she said. "This nest is warm and cozy and sexy too."

The wind slammed into us as we opened the back door and stepped outside. It was a rude, abrupt way to start the day after the warm cocoon we had created inside. I grabbed her hand and we walked across the expanse of meadow over to where the trail began. The wind was less fierce there, weakened a bit by the forest barrier. India took the lead at the entrance to the trail and I focused on our surroundings as we walked, visually marking things I hoped to remember when we came back through with the ATV.

We walked past the rock outcropping and down the steep hill and turned left onto the main part of the trail. I checked my watch, it was 7:30. We should be back at the house by 9:30 at the latest.

The trail was basically the same as the night before, but with more blown-down trees littering the path. After thirty minutes we reached the ravine. We stood on the edge and looked down to where we could see the water cross the trail at the bottom of the ravine. Forty feet of water or more had backed up from the river and was backfilling the ravine. I was surprised the trail hadn't been laid on higher ground circling the ravine.

"Let's go down by the water to get a sense for how deep it is," I said.

We made our way down the steep side of the ravine until we reached the edge of the water. "How deep do you think this is?" I said.

"Maybe two to three feet?"

I took two steps into the water, then three. The water level quickly approached the top of my boots. I could feel the current swirling.

"It's too deep," I said. "Let's go that way," I pointed to the left, "and see where we can cross. The top of my boots is about the same height as the ATV clearance, so when I can cross, it can cross."

We went up the ravine and I waded in periodically. After about 25 yards I was able to cross without having the water come over my boots. We tied reflective tape to a tree to mark the spot.

India looked at me. "This is still too deep for me."

I turned my back to her and crouched. "Hop on."

She got on my back and I waded across, making it easily to the other side. We marked a bush on the other side with tape, then found our way back to the trail. Our pace increased as we got closer to the opening to the house. Just before we were set

99

to clear the tree line, India stopped and turned to me. "Are you good with our plan? I'm scared of what Dad might say or do."

"Our story is that we got up early and left the house to check for damage. It's as simple as that. The only way we have a problem is if he got up in the middle of the night and tried to find you. I think if that is the case, he'll be waiting for us and then I think we play that encounter by ear, because it will take some explaining. Let's be positive and confident and let things fall where they may. I think we'll be fine. First priority once we determine that your Dad isn't here, is for you to take care of your Mom while I call Caleb."

CHAPTER TEN

*"Life every now and then becomes literature, as if
life had been made and not happened."*

—Norman Maclean

The rain had nearly stopped but the sky was still full of torment and the wind was still blowing hard, with gusts up to forty miles an hour. I was glad we weren't going to try to get out today. I didn't see an option for that, whether it was Caleb flying in or me flying out.

We started crossing the wide expanse of lawn to the house. The house looked dark and I didn't see any activity outside, but I couldn't see the shop. India was beside me leaning into the wind, holding onto her hood as she walked beside me across the lawn. We'd both gotten soaked on the trail again, this time not from rain but from the sheets of water whipped from the trees by the wind. We came around the side of the house. The shop doors were open but there was no activity inside. India glanced over at me and I saw the anxiety in her face. We walked the few steps to the backdoor, made it into the mud room, and began to take off our rain gear. The house was silent. Then suddenly the light switched on and Ruth hurried across the kitchen toward us.

"What the hell's going on, India?"

"I'm sorry, Ruth. I'll explain. But first, where's Dad?"

"He and Jacob are over working on the dock."

"Did he say anything about us?"

"No. He seemed generally pissed off but got dressed, drank some coffee, yelled at Jacob to get going, and stomped off. He didn't ask about either one of you. I'm guessing he assumed you were in bed."

"Thank God."

"But what happened? It's nearly 9:45. We were worried sick about you! What the hell?"

"I know. We got a late start last night and it took forever to get over there. The trail is a mess and it took a lot longer than we anticipated. Then we had to check out the plane. So we decided to stay and rest and take the risk that Dad might have discovered we were out all night. It was a better option than trying to come back in the middle of the night, trust me. We wouldn't have gotten back here until 3:00 or 4:00 am, so it was better to rest, come this morning and take the risk that Dad might have discovered we were gone."

"Are we leaving today?"

"No. We're going to give it another day and hope the weather clears. How's Mom?"

"She's not any better. It's hard to say if she's worse, but she's definitely not better. I've been with her every minute that Dad isn't upstairs. She needs to get out of here but Dad's freaking me out. He's just constantly pissed off." She looked at me. "You being here probably isn't helping."

"I'm going upstairs to check on Mom," India said. "Can you make the call to Caleb?" she said to me.

"Sure."

India walked quickly through the kitchen and up the stairs.

Ruth looked at me angrily. "What were you thinking?" she asked. "What the hell?"

"Ruth, I know it sounds crazy but getting over there in a storm like that was way more than we bargained for. And by the time we checked out the plane and got things arranged, it was literally the middle of the night. We needed to sleep somewhere and we also knew we couldn't fly out today in this weather. So we stayed. I still think it was a good idea. I'm sorry. We knew you must have been worrying but that was the best decision at the time."

"Worrying? You have no idea. No idea what it's like to be around my dad on a good day, let alone when he's mad. Now he's pissed as hell. Are we doing this tomorrow? Are we going to make it out?"

"One way or another we'll make it out. Now I better go call Caleb while your dad's out of the house."

I put on my rain gear again even though it wasn't raining and exited through the back door. Halfway to the river I dialed Caleb on the SAT phone.

"Hi Eli," he answered.

"Hi Caleb. Well, the situation is about the same," I said when he answered, "other than the fact it's obvious we're not going today. Our plan is to give it a try tomorrow. What do you think?"

"I've been checking the aviation weather reports out of Anchorage and I hate to say it, but it doesn't look good for me to come over tomorrow either. Coming in from the west, I'd be bucking high winds the whole way. Landing at the Buckleys' would be nearly impossible since it's an east-west oriented runway and I would need north-south in this wind. Anchorage itself looks like it's getting slightly better, but between you and me, it's still dicey. Sorry to tell you this. What's your backup plan?"

"You really want to know?"

"No, but yeah."

"I'm going to fly the Buckleys' plane."

"You're shitting me."

"No, unfortunately I'm not. I soloed a few years ago and had maybe 60 hours in the 172 but I haven't flown a plane in five years and I never got my license."

"You know I could call Anchorage and get you grounded. You can't fly without a license. They'll arrest you when you land – if you land."

"I know. But you won't call Anchorage, because you know we're in a shit storm over here and this could be our only way out."

"Is she really that bad?"

"From what I see, yes.

"Can you get your email?" Caleb asked.

"Yes."

"I think you're making a huge mistake if you do this. I'm still hoping it won't come to that. But just in case, I'm going to send you a preflight checklist, a takeoff checklist and a landing checklist tonight. Print them out and take them with you. I'm also going to send you the correct settings for your fuel richness – it's different up here than where you took your training and you can't make a mistake on that. Lastly, I'm going to send you all of the settings for the balance of your gauges – carb heat, flaps, everything.

"What about India's dad?"

"Nasty, mean, and mad as hell is about all I've seen from him."

"That'll get worse. Hang on and be safe. I'll check the weather again early in the morning and if anything changes, I'll be over. Same plan as before, call me at 9:00 a.m. tomorrow. If you do end up having to fly yourself, take the SAT phone with you and call me when you're ready to leave. I can stay on the phone with you or at least be available while you're in flight."

There was a click at the end of the line and Caleb was gone. I turned and headed back to the house. Halfway across the lawn I saw India coming toward me. The reality of the situation was setting in. For the first time I was panicked.

"Mom's bad. She's in and out of consciousness and hasn't eaten much since we've been here. I took her to the bathroom, and it's like she's a hundred years old. What kind of man doesn't see his wife deteriorating in front of him? I don't know anybody who wouldn't want to do the right thing here, and yet her own husband is blocking her medical care. Fucking unbelievable."

"Do you think she's lucid enough to ask your dad to get her help? Would that influence him?"

"She's lucid enough sometimes but it doesn't matter. I spoke with her about him and she just gave me this melancholy smile. She knows she's powerless over him."

"Shit. I just talked to Caleb. If he can't come tomorrow I honestly don't know what to do," I said, looking at her. "I mean, it won't help if I get us all killed trying to get her to a hospital."

Her eyes welled up with tears and she wiped them away with the back of her hand. The wind was still howling but the rain was gone for now. It was late morning but it was so cloudy the house lights needed to be on. We were standing in the middle of the lawn, maybe fifty yards from the house. I looked past India's shoulder and saw truck lights coming up the hill from the direction of the dock. Jacob and India's dad were coming back for lunch.

"Here comes your dad's truck," I said. "Let's go inside."

India turned to look. "Shit."

We walked quickly back to the house.

"Don't forget. He assumed we were still sleeping when they left. We spent the morning with your mom and this afternoon we're going to try to go fishing, as unlikely as that is in these conditions – he'll think we're on date. At least it buys us some time away from the house and him."

"Okay."

But instead of walking back to the house, India veered off and began heading for the shop. "Better to engage him than to wait," she yelled over her shoulder.

India's dad pulled the truck into the bay on the far-right side of the shop, away from the ATV that Jacob had configured with the frame for the stretcher. Jacob had moved the machine to the back corner and partially covered it so it wouldn't be easily seen. The truck stopped and Jacob got out of the passenger side. He glared at us as he walked around the front of the truck, clearly annoyed. India walked over to greet her dad as he climbed out of the driver's seat.

"How's the dock coming?" she asked.

"We got the footings in and this afternoon we'll start with the planking. Should be done in a couple days. If it weren't for the goddamn weather it would be done by now. Is Mom feeling better? Seemed to me she was starting to turn the corner when I left this morning."

"No, Dad, she's not better. She can only struggle to the bathroom if you hold her up. I don't think that qualifies as getting better."

He looked at her and his eyes darkened with anger.

"I fucking told you I don't need you here micro-managing something that isn't any of your concern. What the hell are you doing here except causing me problems?"

He grabbed a shovel out of the back of the truck and threw it across the shop. It hit one of the other trucks, leaving a sizable dent in the side. He started walking toward India.

Jacob stepped in front of her. "Dad, she's just trying to help – we all are." He put his hand on his father's shoulder. "We all want the best for Mom, but you need to hear our concerns. There are four people in this family, not just you!"

His father shoved Jacob's hand off his shoulder without looking at him and pushed him away. He glared at India, his head tilted, like a bull eyeing a bullfighter. His piercing blue eyes above his full-growth russet beard looked like icicles in a dense forest. I stepped up beside India and he swatted me. "Get out of the way, boy."

India began to back away from him. I grabbed him by the front of his jacket and shoved him against the side of the truck behind us. Jacob grabbed him by the arm. He didn't resist.

"What're you going to do, hit me?" India screamed, walking toward him. I could see that she was in an equal rage. "Where do you get off thinking you control everything that happens around here. You've micromanaged this family for twenty-five years and I'm sick of it, sick of the way you treat us and the way you're treating Mom now. This is no way for a family to operate. And now you're going to hit me?"

Jacob and I were still holding him up against the back of the truck. We were all breathing hard. The father said nothing. He relaxed slightly and we released our hold on him. Jacob and I remained close to him in case he did something unexpected. India was still furious but she said nothing more.

"I've worked my entire life to provide for my family. You and Jacob and Ruth and Mom represent everything I've worked for," he said. "I won't stand by and see us separated and I won't allow mistakes to be made. And moving your mother is a mistake and it won't happen." He looked closely at India. "When the weather clears, you and this," he paused, "*friend*, get back to Caleb's and leave us well enough alone. We can manage from here."

"Fine. But you and I both know Mom had a stroke. I promise you, if anything happens to her under your watch, I'll hold you responsible for the rest of your life."

For a moment I thought she might have decided to give up and go along with what he wanted. But then something in her face let me know she was just trying to pacify her father. We all stood there awkwardly, still breathing heavily from the adrenaline coursing through us, looking from one to another.

"Let's go," India snapped at me. She turned and started heading for the back door. I looked at Jacob and her dad, then turned and followed her.

As we were crossing the lawn I glanced back at the shop. Both men were moving around, putting tools away and reloading the truck with more planks for the dock.

⟨───⟩

The aroma of Ruth's cooking was welcoming inside the house. We hadn't eaten anything since dinner last night and I was starving. India started taking off her gear in the mudroom. She kept her head down, averting her eyes from Ruth's gaze. I took my gear off too and stowed it on the shelf above the coats, ready for whatever was coming next.

Ruth came out to the hallway. "What's going on?"

"We're sticking with the plan for tomorrow," India responded. "He's out of his fucking mind and we need to get her out of here. How's she doing?"

"No better."

"We just need to go about the rest of the day as normal. He thinks we'll leave when the weather clears, which we will, technically, but not in the manner he thinks. He believes Eli and I are just going to go away and leave everything the way it is here. I'm going upstairs to see Mom. Has she eaten?"

"A little. Some cereal and a banana. More than yesterday. But I can tell the pain in her shoulder is terrible, and we're almost out of pain pills."

India kissed Ruth on the cheek, then turned and headed upstairs. Ruth and I went into the kitchen.

"How bad was it?" she asked.

"Ruth, how old are you?"

"Seventeen."

"I'm sorry about this – you're too young to have to be involved in all this crap."

"It's not an age thing. You don't know what it's like being raised in this environment. On the one hand, we have the freest existence in the world. We have thousands of acres to explore and the license to do it. But on the other hand, we come home to a tyrant, an extremist who keeps doing the worst possible thing by us, which is to try to control our minds. It hasn't worked and that's a good thing, but it's exhausting to go through this every day of your life. The lies, the fabrications, the acting as if you agree with a deranged mind just to get through the day. I may be only seventeen, but I've seen enough nonsense for a lifetime. Today is just another chapter."

She looked up at me and tears filled her eyes. I realized how beautiful she was.

Long blond hair and eyes as blue as the sky. And she was clearly the most innocent of the bunch, the one you'd figure to be least prepared for this. Yet here she was with a clear perspective, maybe the clearest perspective of the whole family. I remember being so happy to know her at that moment.

I put my arms around her and she hugged me hard. Over her shoulder I saw Jacob walking with purpose toward the back door.

"Here comes your brother," I whispered to Ruth. She turned, began wiping her eyes as she went into the half-bath off the kitchen, and closed the door behind her. Jacob burst into the mudroom.

"Jesus, I can't believe that just happened," he said. "That scene out in the shop."

"Neither can I."

"Where's India?"

"Upstairs with your mom. What's going on with your dad now?"

"He asked me to get some sandwiches so we can get back to work on the dock. Where's Ruth?"

"Right here," Ruth said, walking into the kitchen from the bathroom and moving toward the stove.

"Dad wants some sandwiches so we can get back to work. I don't think he wants to come in here."

"I heard. Give me a sec and I'll give you some burgers and a thermos of soup."

I heard footsteps coming down the stairs and India came into the kitchen. The four of us stood in a circle and Ruth began preparing packages for Jacob and her Dad.

"We need to go with our plan for tomorrow morning," India said. "Mom's in bad shape and we're almost out of pain pills. I have no idea what's going on with her head or stroke or whatever but it's not getting better. I think she needs surgery on her shoulder and a stroke protocol. This may be the last time we can talk as a group. So Jacob, you have to get Dad out of here tomorrow morning as planned so we can start getting Mom ready to go to the Buckleys'. Then as soon as you can, you need to hightail it back here so you can help us get Mom onto the ATV and come with us on the trail. You'll have to come up with some excuse for leaving Dad."

India paused and looked at Ruth. "Ruth, unfortunately, you can't come with us. There would be too much weight in the plane with all of us. Can you handle things here with Dad alone? You'd just say you knew nothing about what we were up to. Can you manage that?" India asked.

"Of course," Ruth said from the sink. She looked like she might be blinking back tears.

India's face softened, then she looked at Jacob.

"Jacob, when you leave with Dad in the morning, we'll get the ATV pulled up close to the house, get Mom ready, and hopefully get her downstairs. When you get back, we'll rig the stretcher and use your help getting her onto the ATV, ready for the crossing to the Buckleys'. Eli is going to call Caleb tomorrow morning. If he can fly in and help us, he will. If not, Eli's going to fly us to Anchorage. In the meantime, everything needs to be normal or as normal as things can be. I'm going to take Eli to Ralston Creek today, assuming the rain continues to hold off. So we'll all be separated, and Dad shouldn't think anything's strange and that we're just waiting out the weather. Sound good?"

"No, not really. But I guess it's a plan," Jacob said.

Ruth turned and handed Jacob a packet of burgers and thermos of soup.

"And whatever you do, make sure you don't finish the dock today," I added. "Because that's our ticket out of here tomorrow morning."

CHAPTER ELEVEN

⸻

"Blessed are the hearts that can bend; they shall never be broken."

—Albert Camus

Jacob left the kitchen to return to his dad. India and I were standing alone with Ruth. "I'm going back upstairs with Mom," Ruth said. "What're you guys going to do?"

"When all else fails, go fishing," India said. She turned to me and for the first time since last night, her face seemed more relaxed. "There're a couple rods in the basement. Grab those and some fly's and I'll show you where I learned to fly fish," she said. "Ruth, you okay holding down the fort with Mom for a few hours?"

"Of course, no problem."

"Okay, the rods are in the corner of the basement across from where your cot is. There's a small box of flies next to them. I'll fix us some lunch and get a thermos of coffee and we'll take the other ATV and head out. It's about a 30-minute ride from here," she said.

"Great." I answered as I turned and went downstairs to the bed that I hadn't yet slept in. I grabbed the rods and fly's and slipped on a fresh pair of jeans, pulled on another fleece shirt and an outer jacket. It had stopped raining and was sunny, but the wind hadn't stopped blowing and was as intense as last night. Impossible flying and fishing conditions, but at least the fishing trip would get us out of the house and away from her Dad. I was in.

We slipped on light down jackets but left the rain gear behind for once and walked out the back door and over to the shop. I had the rods and fly's. India was carrying a backpack with the food, and a shotgun slung over her shoulder. We found the ATV and strapped the rods to the front cargo area. She handed me the gun and backpack and she stepped onto the machine and started it up. Once it was idling, she motioned for me to get on and I sat behind her with the backpack snug on my shoulders and the gun at the ready.

"Hold on." She said as we backed out of the shop. Within seconds, we were moving across the wide lawn toward the deep forest at the very back of the property, an area I hadn't seen before. As I looked over her shoulder, I scanned the forest for an opening but didn't see anything obvious. We were moving fast. Obviously, she knew her way around an ATV.

As we approached the forest, she turned her head slightly. "Hold on. It's going to get bumpy when we hit the trail."

I was already holding onto her waist with my left hand as I held onto the gun in my right. I nudged myself forward onto the seat, so we were packed tightly together and I moved my left arm completely around her waist, not knowing where we were headed or what "bumpy" meant.

As we neared the forest wall, I could just make out a sliver of an opening in the dense bush. She slowed the vehicle slightly as we dipped down into a small ditch, then moved up the other side and slid into the opening. We were immediately enveloped in dense woods much like what we experienced on the way to the Buckleys' last night; but the trail itself was better maintained and there didn't appear to be any water issues. Once we were firmly on the trail, she turned on the headlight and accelerated along the trail. As far as I could see ahead of us, the trail was straight and mostly level and didn't have the mass of downed branches and brush tangles that last night's trail had.

We drove for 20 minutes before we came to a wide turn to the left where the trail sloped downward. Once we hit the steepest part of the downslope, she began to back off the speed a bit. I could just make out a stream near the bottom of the trail and figured we were getting close to the fishing spot.

At the bottom of the hill, she turned right into a small clearing and slowed the vehicle to a stop. "Okay, we're going to turn left up here and drive a few yards down a rough trail to a little parking area, then we'll hike along the river up to a spot where we'll start fishing," she said over the noise of the engine. She drove the vehicle up the path and into a make shift parking area beside the stream and turned it off. It was immediately silent. The only sound was the rushing stream beside us and the wind blowing through the stand of Jack and Norway pines.

I helped her unfasten the rods and grabbed the fly box. She took the backpack, put it over her shoulders, picked up the gun and chambered a round then looked over at me.

"How about lunch? I'm starving," she said.

"Sounds good. How far up is the first hole?"

"A hundred yards or so. We'll be having lunch and some delicious coffee in no more than fifteen minutes."

"Perfect, let's go."

We walked along the stream as the afternoon sunlight played off the water, creating a myriad of prisms and sparkles dancing off it as we walked. We were in brilliant sunlight and the day was spectacular - other than the wind, which was still gusting over 40 mph. We were mostly protected in the valley alongside the creek. The old trail we were on meandered alongside the stream.

So, this was where she started fishing. I could see the attraction. It was remote, protected and the stream itself was narrow, so it would be easy to make a cast completely across it. Perfect place to learn and perfect the craft. She was showing me her sacred place. A place that all fly fisherman have. Their water.

After fifteen minutes, we reached an opening in the trail where the forest wall pushed back 30 yards from the stream. In the middle of the opening was a huge flat boulder probably 15 feet wide and six feet tall, with indentations on the side that you could use as footholds. She climbed up and rested her pack and the gun on top. I leaned the rods up against the side of the rock and climbed up beside her. She looked over at me and took off her baseball hat. I could see her hair sticking to the side of her face – wet with sweat. It was the first time I had really looked at her since last night. We had been engulfed in chaos all day and now we had a respite and were at her secret place. We could finally take some time to relax.

"Let's start with some coffee," she said.

"This place is beautiful, India. This is better than any place we have fished this week and that's saying a lot, especially given the spring creek. Thanks for bringing me here. I think this is your place, these are your waters."

"This is home. This is me. This is where my soul lives."

"I'm honored you're showing me this. I'm not sure I've ever seen a place quite so beautiful. I'd like to bottle this and take it with me."

"Just plan to come back here with me someday and you won't have to bottle it. I'm happy to share."

She opened the backpack and brought out the thermos. We were off the ground with a perfect view of the river. Our feet dangled off the edge of the boulder as we drank our coffee and looked out over the water.

She moved closer to me, so we were touching. It was chilly with the wind and we were just barely warm enough in our light coats. I looked over at her and she smiled. "I know I said last night how much I appreciate everything you've done for me but I need to say it again. You're a gentleman and thanks for helping me in the shop and with everything else for that matter. I'm horrified that I've put you in this position. I hardly know you and look what you're doing for me. Nobody wants to air their dirty family laundry, let alone do it with someone you've just met."

"Honestly, I couldn't have imagined in my wildest dreams what's taken place the past few days," I replied. "All kidding aside, I'm in a state of shock over what we've been doing; but with that said, we'll get through this. That's the one thing I've learned in life – things do work out in spite of how bad they look and how much you think they won't work out."

She looked up at me and tears filled her eyes. "And assuming we get through this, what happens next?"

"I haven't a clue," I said. "I hope like I've never hoped for anything that there's more for us. Right now, though, I feel as though you are the only woman I've ever known."

She put her arm around my waist and lay her head on my shoulder. I put my arm around her and moved us closer together on the rock. With the sunshine and the relief from being removed from the chaos back at the house, we began to relax - and in our sheltered little valley I grew tired as the sun baked us. Neither one of us talked, just held on to each other.

After a few minutes her body went slack, and her breathing grew heavy. I gently woke her and made a soft makeshift bed with an extra jacket and fleece. I laid everything down on the rock then motioned for her to lay down. We were both exhausted, but her more than me. She laid down on the pile of clothes in the warm sunshine and in moments she was fast asleep. I sat on the rock and covered her the best I could, then got into the pack again and pulled out the thermos. I needed more coffee.

After a while, as India slept, I got off the rock and approached the stream. As I walked up to it, it was luminescent. Gin clear water, virtually transparent, and no more than two feet deep in any spot. I could see the rainbows sitting in the deeper pockets facing upstream - all competing for the limited food sources this high up and in such a small, fast stream. I cast my fly carefully upstream and time and again it was caught in the fast current and washed back down upon me, the line crumpled at my feet. The float was incredibly fast. Finally, after numerous attempts, I floated my fly down onto a section of calm water just off the main current on the other side of the steam. I held my rod high, well above my head so as not to get my line on the water and did an upstream mend. It was a perfect float. The water boiled just downstream from my fly and in an instant, a large rainbow rose and took my fly. I set the hook and the fish was off downstream in a flash. I was just off the shoreline in the edge of the water on the other side of the stream from the fish and it took five minutes to strip it in across the fast current. I admired it the entire way into my net, the rainbow coloring on its side as brilliant as a Spring painting. Just as I landed it, I heard a rustling behind me, looked over and saw India standing streamside behind me, a cup of coffee in her hand and a smile on her face.

"Nice fish."

"Thanks. I could fish here all day, or maybe for eternity."

"You're becoming an Alaskan, Mr. New York."

"I think I've always been an Alaskan. It just took me a while to find it. I'm a slow learner."

"Let's have lunch," she said as she began to walk back to the rock. I released the fish and followed her and we were soon sitting again with our legs dangling off the edge, eating sandwiches and drinking coffee - our bodies touching as we ate in silence in the brilliant sunshine.

After lunch and more fishing, we finally went back to the rock, watching as the late afternoon sky descended upon us, rain clouds now lingering just off in the distance and the wind still bending the pines at their tops.

"It's getting late, I think we should spend a half hour more on the stream and then head back. I don't want to leave Ruth alone too long and I want to get there before Dad and Jacob get back."

"Agreed," I said

After catching a few more fish, we walked back down the trail to the ATV, loaded our gear, and started off on the ride back. The forest was now suddenly more alive. The wind seemed to disrupt the wildlife and there was activity everywhere. Everything seemed to be in motion – the birds, squirrels and all manner of forest life afoot. As if the wind was telling every living thing to hurry about his task for the day. It was busy.

We finally emerged from the forest and the house and shop were in sight. India sped across the lawn and everything seemed to be in the same order as when we left. We turned the corner towards the shop. Jacob and his Dad were nowhere to be seen. We assumed they were still be working on the dock. We parked the ATV, grabbed our gear and hurried into the house.

The kitchen was quiet. We stowed our gear and poured ourselves what was left of the morning's coffee. We heard soft footsteps coming down the stairs, and Ruth came around the corner.

"How is she?" India asked.

"I actually think she's a bit more lucid. Still confused and loses her track of mind but overall, I think her mental state is better. But her shoulder is worse and we only have three pain pills left."

"Three pills left means her last pill is noon tomorrow," India said, looking over at me.

I just nodded. Our situation was getting worse and our options of getting out no better. It may actually come down to me flying that plane and that wasn't a good alternative. The reality began to sink in. I would be responsible for three lives other than my own, I hadn't flown a plane in years and most importantly, I didn't have a license.

CHAPTER TWELVE

"For it was not into my ear you whispered, but into my heart. It was not my lips you kissed, but my soul."

—Judy Garland

I checked my watch after a fitful night's sleep. It was 6:30 a.m. The basement was jet black and chilly. I pulled the quilt up around my chin and rolled onto my side. I heard footsteps in the kitchen above me. Muffled voices sounded like they were in the mud room. Maybe it was Jacob and his dad getting ready to go out to the dock. I'd wait a few more minutes and see what happened.

The sounds above me stopped at around 6:45. Jacob and his dad had probably left to start their work for the day. I felt a pit in my stomach. Today was the day we would make a break for Anchorage and I had a feeling that Caleb wouldn't be flying in to save us.

Last night when everyone was asleep I'd gone into the den and used the computer to download Caleb's sectional maps of approach routes into the Lake Hood airport in Anchorage and his fuel settings. Hood was adjacent to Anchorage International; it had both water and land airstrips. I'd flown in and out of Hood many times over the years, but only as a passenger. Last night I'd also downloaded as much information as I could find about flying a Cessna 172. I wasn't confident I could fly us safely into Anchorage, but I did recognize all the items on the checklists.

At 7 a.m. the door to the basement opened, light seeped in from the kitchen, and then the basement door quickly closed. I lifted my head and saw India's legs as she started down the stairs. It was still dark in the basement and I turned on my cell phone flashlight and shone it up to her. She was dressed in flannel pajamas with a long sweater on top. She came over to my bed, bent down and kissed me then pulled back the covers, and slipped in beside me. I made room for her. She was facing me.

"Good morning," she whispered.

"Good morning. Did I hear Jacob and your dad leaving?"

"Yeah. I stayed in bed until they left so I wouldn't create any more issues with dad. He sounded calm this morning from what I could hear so I decided to let it go."

"Probably a good idea."

She had her hands around my waist and she inserted her leg between mine. She kissed me again, this time it was longer and deeper and I could taste the toothpaste she had just used to brush her teeth. Her breathing became more rapid and she pulled herself into me. I adjusted my position so I could move on top of her, rolling her over so her head was now resting on the pillow below me. In the darkness I could just make out her features. I ran my hands under her pajamas and up to her breast. Her nipples were hard. She pushed her crotch into me as we kissed again. I pushed my hand deep into her crotch and squeezed and she moaned softly, her head sinking back into the pillow as she arched her back. She reached down and slipped off her pajama bottoms then untied the waistband of mine and I felt them slip away as she worked them lower on my waist. I unbuttoned her shirt and suddenly she was naked beneath me, her chest rising and falling in deeper, more passionate breaths.

I moved on top of her and she spread her legs and moved me into her. She was moist and I entered her easily, the makeshift bed squeaking and creaking as our pace increased. She was moaning softly, kissing me and running her fingers through my hair, me now pounding her and I could hear her breath coming in short gasps as she neared climax, her fingers pinching into my back.

"Oh God," she whispered into my ear as her entire body shuddered, then arched up. I continued my wicked pace, now too far gone to stop. Beyond the point of no return, I came deep inside her. We were soaked, our skin slick on each other and I could smell her aroma beneath me. I laid down on top of her then slid off beside her, both of us now facing up into the darkness of the basement. Our breathing slowly returning to normal.

She lay still. I could hear her breathing but didn't look over. India didn't offer anything but grabbed my hand beneath the blanket and our fingers intertwined as we lay in that cold basement. I listened to the sound of the wind blowing and watched a yellow dawn breaking, through the basement window.

"India?" Ruth called down into the still-dark basement where we had fallen asleep after our lovemaking. India jerked awake beside me. She had rolled onto her side, her naked back side facing me. She brought the covers further on top of her.

"Yes, Ruth. We'll be up in a few minutes. Everything okay?"

"That's a relative question, but yes. I just wondered where you were."

Ruth closed the basement door. India put her leg over mine and moved closer, our noses nearly touching.

"You ready for this?" she said.

"I'm not sure I've been ready for anything that's happened to me since I got here a week ago. So yes, what's another day in Alaska."

She laughed. The light in the basement was now a lighter yellow, just beginning its slow reluctant transition to daylight. I could just begin to make out her emerald-green eyes. Framed by her auburn hair, her face looked unusually beautiful in the amber light of the basement. She put her elbow on the pillow, propped her head up with her hand, and looked at me intently.

"We'll have to write a second chapter in this book sometime soon after we get Mom handled in Anchorage," she said.

"I'm more worried about what comes next for us than I am about getting your mom to Anchorage. I know that sounds crazy, but that's how I feel."

"I know."

She lay back on the pillow and nuzzled my neck, breathing deep, calm breaths.

Finally she stirred and sat up on the edge of the bed, still naked. "I guess it's time to go," she said. She stood up pulled on her pants, tied the waist and after a moment, pulled on her shirt, put her hair behind her ears, and looked down at me.

"Let's go."

In the kitchen Ruth was at the stove as usual, preparing breakfast. She glanced over at us and gave a knowing smile.

"Well, good morning," she said.

"Hi Ruth." I said.

India walked over and put her arms around her sister. "Good morning. How's Mom?"

"I think her mind is better, but her shoulder is worse. We're down to two pills. She'll be out of pills by nightfall and that'll be bad. The pain's terrible."

"Okay, we'll get her out of here today one way or another. Thanks for making breakfast – we'll need it. Let's eat as much as we can, then get started with this madness. I'm going up to check on Mom and get ready. I'll be right back." India looked over at me. I waved my coffee cup in response and sat at the kitchen table. Ruth looked over her shoulder and gave a sly smile.

"What, Ruth?"

"How'd you two sleep?" she asked.

"You're funny this morning."

"I was just thinking that if this were a different time—different circumstances— you'd be the best thing that's ever happened to my sister. But then I realized that it doesn't matter what the setting or the circumstances are. You're still the best thing. Thanks for taking care of us."

"You're welcome. I'm not really sure I'm taking care of you, but thanks anyway."

"Nobody gets to India. There's never been anyone serious. She's too smart and complicated. You're in deep with her. You should consider yourself lucky, or I guess unlucky as the case may be."

"I wonder why that is?"

"What?"

"Why she hasn't found anyone. She's got to be the most beautiful woman up here other than you. Why hasn't it happened for her?"

"I'm just guessing here, but maybe the same reason it hasn't happened for you?"

"Are you sure you're just seventeen?"

"Like I said, we grow up fast here in the bush. But whatever. I just think the two of you are a dangerous match – a good match, mind you, but dangerous nonetheless. You're both too smart, too evolved, too good looking, too complicated. But if there was a way to make it come together, and I think the odds against that are better than the odds for it, you would be one awesome couple."

"You're a wise woman, Ruth. I'm so happy I got to meet you. Regardless of what happens here, let's not lose touch, okay?"

"Deal."

Just then India rounded the bend at the bottom of the stairs. A quick change. She was dressed for the day – jeans, a shirt with a sweatshirt over it, a bandana around her neck. Her hair was in a long braid falling down her back to her waist. She had just a hint of makeup on for the first time. She looked fresh and ready. She glanced at the two of us and smiled.

"What's this about not losing touch?"

"Ruth and I just agreed that we need to keep in touch after this episode is over. We're thinking of each other as extended family and it feels good to us," I said.

"Is that right?" India asked.

"Yeah. Now sit down and let's have breakfast," Ruth said.

We all sat around the small kitchen table and ate the artful breakfast Ruth had prepared. An egg and sausage frittata with peppers, onions, cheese, and a healthy dose of fresh kale from the garden. We ate in silence, devouring the food as if we hadn't eaten in weeks.

"Okay," India said when we were finished. "Mom's mind is better but her shoulder's worse. I think we have a better shot at this if we don't use the stretcher. I'll drive the ATV and she can hold onto me with her good arm. Eli, you sit behind her and we'll essentially sandwich her between the two of us. The jarring ride won't be easy or good, but we'll give her the last two pills at the same time so she has a double dose of painkillers," India said, looking over at me.

"What about crossing the spot where the trail meets the water and it's impassable. How are we going to get her around the ravine?"

"Jacob's coming with us on the other ATV. He'll walk ahead on that section and clear as much brush and trees as he can with the machete so we can follow on his path. I know it's a mess in there but I think we can make it work," she said, looking at me intently. "The ravine gets shallow enough to cross after about 70 yards."

"Okay. I agree that it's better to have your mom sit on the ATV between us than for her to lie in a hammock. We need to fashion a sling for her arm to immobilize her shoulder as much as possible. Ruth, do you think you could create something that literally plasters her arm against her chest?"

"Yeah, I have a bunch of old shirts I use for rags. I can tie them together and make something that should help."

"Perfect, we've got two hours until Jacob gets back," India said. "So we need to move. Eli, you pull the ATV over here by the house and I'll let Mom know what we're up to. I'll get her up, and cleaned up a bit and dressed. Let's start the process of getting her downstairs at around nine-thirty, then get her coat on and get her outside so we can have her ready to go at ten a.m. sharp."

We looked at each other around the table. There was an unspoken acknowledgement that we were in over our heads but momentum was moving in the direction of executing our plan. We were now officially co-conspirators against their dad.

At nine-thirty, India, Ruth and I gathered at their mom's bedside. She was sitting on top of the sheets wearing a pair of black leggings and a brown-and-red top that extended over her waist. She looked clean and her hair was neatly brushed. Her injured shoulder and arm were in a sling that held them tight against her chest. She looked over at me and smiled, looking much better than the last time I saw her, although occasionally she rubbed her shoulder with her free hand. I had heard that some doctors do less rather than more in terms of treatment for some mild stroke victims. Maybe that would be the case with her.

"Mom, we're ready to go. Are you ready?" India asked.

Her mom nodded.

"Okay, let's go," India said. She began to move her mom's legs over the side of the bed. I put my arms around her waist, careful not to bump her shoulder, and together India and I helped her off the bed. She put her good arm around India's shoulder. We slowly moved to the end of the bed and I led the way down the hall to the stairs. Ruth took her place on the other side of her mom and she and India carefully helped her out of the bedroom and down the hall.

At the staircase we stopped to regroup. India looked down the stairs and then over at me.

"I think it's best if I carry her," I said. "That's the safest option. I can cradle her in my arms and then we wouldn't put any stress on her shoulder and won't have to worry about anyone falling."

India looked concerned but nodded. Her mom was still quiet, as was Ruth.

"Helen, I know this whole thing is strange for you, and believe me, it's even stranger for me. I'm sorry we haven't met under different circumstances. I'm going to take care of you and get you to a hospital today. The first challenge we'll face is me carrying you down these stairs, so please just trust me and relax and we'll be fine. Okay?" I said.

"Okay," she whispered.

I turned her around so her bad shoulder was facing away from me, put my arm around the middle of her back and my other arm around the back of her knees and gently rolled her up into my arms, picking up her legs as her upper torso slid against my chest. She weighed nothing. She laid her head against my chest and I turned and walked carefully and slowly down the stairs, through the house, and over to the back door. I set her down on the bench in the mud room.

It took us fifteen minutes to get her dressed for the cold. We put her coat on over her shoulders and buttoned it in the front. I picked her up again and carried her down the outside steps and gently put her side saddle on the ATV. With two pain pills in her, she was groggy but mostly pain free. By my calculations, we had about eight hours before the pills wore off – more than enough time to get to the Buckleys.

Once we were loaded, Ruth came over and kissed each of us on the cheek, her eyes welling with tears. She looked at her mom. "Mom, I love you so much. I'll see you soon in Anchorage." Her mom nodded, reached out with her good hand, and patted Ruth's cheek.

Then we moved Helen's leg over the saddle and India and I got on with her, India driving and me in the rear, with Helen sandwiched between us. India started the ATV and took off slowly toward the trail that led to the Buckleys' house. The lawn was smoother than the trail was going to be, and Helen was packed in tightly and didn't complain. Jacob came up beside us on the other ATV and motioned for us to stop just as we got to the opening to the trail.

"We're about done with the dock. I did as we discussed – I intentionally forgot the air compressor for the nail gun. So I had an excuse to come back, but he's pissed off. He spent all morning complaining about everyone and when I don't return in half an hour he'll be charging back over and be on our tail soon. I don't think we have much time to get to the Buckleys' and get out of here."

Just then I realized I had forgotten to call Caleb and the SAT phone was in the house.

"Shit. I forgot to call Caleb. Jacob, you're going to have to go back to the house and call him and see if he can make it in."

"You're kidding me, right? You forgot to call him?"

"No, I'm not kidding and yes, I forgot. Get back there as quickly as possible and then join us. And come fast. We're going to need your help at the ravine if not before."

Jacob handed me his machete, spun his ATV around, and fired off in the direction of the house. India restarted our ATV and moved forward toward the opening in the forest and the trail that lay beyond.

We were moving slowly, maybe five miles an hour. There were ruts and downed branches and limbs littering the trail. We were mostly silent, though Helen occasionally moaned in pain. India stopped every few hundred yards to readjust us. I could see the trail begin to disappear downward and I knew the ravine was getting close. This would be the hard part.

As we crested the top of the hill that dropped into the ravine, India stopped the ATV and got off. I pulled some water out of the backpack and we all took a drink. India gave her mom three Advil to help with the pain. I walked down the hill to check out the ravine. I was surprised Jacob hadn't caught up with us yet but I didn't want to wait for him.

The water at the bottom of the ravine had receded from yesterday, but it still looked too deep to cross. I scoped out a new course through the forest and around the water that looked slightly better. It was closer to the trail but would work now that the water level was lower. It seemed like our best option. I took the machete and began to work a path, cutting the majority of the blowdown out of our way for the first portion of the route.

When I rejoined India and her mom back at the ATV Helen was alert and awake but had a pained expression on her face. We needed to keep moving and get this over with.

We began moving carefully through the forest, with India driving and me walking ahead, moving larger branches out of the way so the ATV could ride as smoothly as possible. We reached a few dense brush piles that we had to circumnavigate, tilting the ATV and requiring Helen to hold on tightly to India and to adjust her seating. Finally we came to an area that looked like we could cross the water. I motioned India to stop, then I waded out into the water to test the depth and see how muddy the bottom was. It was deeper than what I wanted but the bottom was firm. I thought we could cross. I returned to the parked ATV.

"I think we can cross here."

India looked at me desperately.

"It's all good," I said. "We can do this. We're almost there."

I walked back to the water. India started the machine and crept along behind me. As we entered the water the ground leveled out, so it was easier for Helen to sit. The ATV crept along behind me as we made it across the fifteen-foot wide ravine and then gingerly crept up the bank on the opposite side. We had made the crossing.

We turned left so we were headed back in the direction of the trail. I found a game trail that was fairly level and we worked our way back to the main trail. It took 25 minutes total to complete the crossing.

We were now back on the main trail and were essentially home free. India stopped and we all got off and regrouped before the last push. We each took a drink of water, then with India's assistance Helen walked around the ATV a few times and stretched to the extent she was able.

"Everyone ready to go?" I asked.

Helen nodded and we carefully got her back on the ATV, with India once again in the driver's seat and me bringing up the rear behind Helen. We started up the half-mile incline that opened onto Buckleys' lawn. The trail was much better here so we were able to move slightly faster. Still no Jacob, though. I checked behind us period-ically to see if he was coming. Nothing. Chances were good that their dad suspected something, because otherwise Jacob would have been here by now. Occasionally India looked behind us as she drove – no doubt feeling the same concern I was.

The wind was picking up again and it had started to drizzle. Storm clouds were lacing in from the west and I could see some thunderheads off in the distance. The wind was starting to howl through the trees, bending them nearly in half. Not a good omen for Caleb getting in or us getting out. It was 10:15 a.m.

We crested the final rise, turned a sharp corner around the rock outcropping, and were on the Buckleys' lawn, just a hundred yards or so from the cluster of buildings.

India stopped the machine and looked back at me.

"Where the hell is Jacob?"

"No idea."

"What should we do?"

"Go to the house and make a plan."

With that she turned and we took off across the lawn. India wasn't being as careful with the speed, and Helen was moaning under her breath even though I was still holding her around the waist and keeping her pinned between India and me, but still the speed was making the ride rough.

Finally, we arrived at the house. I got off the ATV first, then India, then we helped Helen get off carefully and slowly. The ride had done her no good. She was in obvious pain and we were out of pills. I'd thought the ones she took earlier would last until the evening, but the ride was just too rough. We needed to get her settled before we attempted anything further.

"Let's go inside and get your mom comfortable," I said over the wind, which was blowing harder now. The cloud cover was at tree-top level and the drizzle was picking up. India put her arm around her mom while I held open the door and we ushered her inside and directly over to the living room sofa. We set her down slowly and carefully leaned her back against the pillows with her feet up, so she was lying completely flat.

Helen looked up at India and smiled weakly. "Sweetie, I love you. But this may be too much for us," she whispered. "I'm not sure how much more I can take and your dad is sure to find us. It's hard to outsmart that man. And when he finds us it's going to be so bad. You know that."

"Mom, if it's the last thing I do I'm getting you to a hospital. We'll rest here for as long as necessary. I think you should try to get some sleep and when you wake up we'll have a bite to eat. We'll have a plan of action in place by then. Okay?"

Helen looked up and whispered, "Okay sweetie." Then her eyes closed and she fell instantly asleep.

India covered her up more completely and motioned me into the kitchen.

"We're screwed. Where the hell is Jacob and what are we going to do now? We clearly can't move her in this condition and we also can't wait or my dad is going to figure this out. I'm freaking out!"

"I'm betting the reason Jacob isn't here is that your dad came back to the house and realized we're gone. I'm also convinced that Jacob and Ruth won't give us up and will create a cover story. The bad news is that there are only a few places where we could have gone on an ATV. What are the other ones besides here?" I asked.

"There are three other homesteads in the area besides ours. This is the closest but also the place we go to the least frequently. We are friendly with the Buckleys but not close. They've always thought my dad was crazy and didn't disguise it. I think this is a place he would look, but maybe not first…unless he thought about the plane."

"Where are the others?"

"They're in the opposite direction and a little farther from our house than here. I'm not sure, but I think his instinct might be to try the other places first. They're completely off the grid like our house, so there's no way out there except for the river. This is the only place with plane access, but he may think we'd try a river escape because it's an obvious choice. Who knows?"

"First things first. Let's search this house and see if they have any pain pills. Either way we're going to have to do something about Helen's pain come tonight. Then we'll think about how to get out of here and when."

India went toward the back of the house where the bedrooms and bathrooms were. I searched the half-bath off the kitchen as well as the pantry that held emergency lights, batteries, and all manner of supplies. I found an emergency first aid kit on the lower shelf there. I opened it up and found a pill bottle with five pills in it. The old prescription label was faded but sure enough, the pills were Percocet. India came back with prescription- strength Tylenol.

We might be in business on the pain front.

CHAPTER THIRTEEN

*"Life is not a problem to be solved, but a reality
to be experienced."*

—Kierkegaard

India set about looking for provisions in the Buckleys' pantry and found a plentiful supply of canned goods and soups, as well as a freezer full of moose, beef, and pork. We could survive if we weren't found. She made her Mom some green tea and we got her up to use the restroom. We were fortunate the Buckleys and everyone else in the bush kept their homes functional when they weren't there. We turned the baseboard heat up to 75 degrees and the house warmed quickly.

I moved the ATV into the hangar with the plane so it wouldn't be noticeable if anyone came to the house or arrived via the river. Then I checked the plane again. It was just as we had left it, and the bed we'd made in the rear looked more than adequate. I took the Anchorage sectional maps and checklists from my pack, sat in the plane, and ran through all of the lists.

I found a lock in the hangar with the combination written on a small piece of paper on the back. I wrote the numbers on my palm, removed the code from the lock, and locked the hangar door as I left. I walked back into the house to the smell of a huge pot of soup on the stove. It was one-thirty in the afternoon.

India and I stood in the kitchen.

"I sat with Mom for a while and fed her some soup and water and gave her one of the Percocet's. She went to the restroom and now she's out again. I think the Percocet is still good. I'm concerned about moving her today. That's bad news on many fronts because the longer we wait, the better the chances are of us being found here." She leaned back against the counter and looked up at me.

"I agree. If we can't move her then we can't. It's also a shitty day – the weather's deteriorating again and the ceilings are getting worse. Not as bad as they were a couple of days ago but still bad. I'm thinking we're on a bit of an island here with no Jacob and no knowledge of what's happening, but it's probably safe to assume your dad is trying to find us. Even so, I think at this point our only choice is to stay here for the rest of the day and night and try to get out tomorrow morning. We can stay hidden as best as we can. Let's hope your dad searches other homesteads first or gets too drunk to go anywhere, at least until tomorrow. I don't think we have any other options, do you?"

"Not really. I guess at this point we leave when we have a weather window, and that comes down to you and your judgment. In the meantime, I'll try to see what bedrooms are the most remote and inaccessible from the outside of the house and hope if Dad shows up he just looks in and leaves. Did we leave any tracks outside?"

"I checked. It doesn't look that bad. They have flagstone pavers everywhere so you really can't see any tracks. I think if we turn off every light and hide as deep in the house as we can, he won't be inclined to think we're here. But of course, if he's in a rage it won't matter. He'll break the door down and we're toast.

"And by the way, I'm starving," I said.

"I found a pot of chicken noodle soup and defrosted it and it's fantastic. Remind me to thank the Buckleys when I see them."

I sat at the kitchen table and India joined me. The weather outside was windy with low threatening clouds. I guessed the sustained surface wind speed was 15 miles an hour gusting to 20, with much higher winds at elevation. That would be problematic for me to fly in. I ate the soup and we sat in silence for a few minutes.

"As much as I'd like to diminish the seriousness of our situation, I can't," I said. "And, to make matters worse, I don't like it that we're essentially cut off from the outside world," I said. "We have no phones, no radios, nothing to let us know what's happening. We don't know what the weather is here or in Anchorage, where Caleb is, or where Jacob and your father are. Nothing. And we have a sick woman with us who can't take care of herself. Let's think about options to try to make the most informed decision possible."

"Okay," she said.

"As I see it, we have maybe three options. First, we could try to fly out tomorrow, but that assumes the weather is good here and also in Anchorage because again, we don't know what weather is anywhere but where we are, and it also assumes I can fly the plane safely and that we're not found before tomorrow. Second, we could try to leverage the river somehow. There's a boat in the hangar and we could try that option, hoping that the river is better after a day or so of little rain. I don't know where we could go, but I'm assuming you do. Third, we could go back, admit we made a huge mistake, and pay the consequences. We could apologize, and he would probably just kick us out. But of course, we wouldn't have solved the problem with your mom. Anything I'm missing?"

"We're not going back. That's not an option. You don't know my dad. He would be in such a rage it wouldn't be safe. Something bad could happen and Mom could die. He'd never forgive me for the rest of my life."

"But he won't forgive you anyway. What do you think he's going to do when he finds out we're in Anchorage? He'll be beside himself, and, from what you tell me, he could even be crazier when he finds us there."

"He can't go that crazy at a hospital. There's security, and the Anchorage police know Dad. He's smart enough to not do something violent at the hospital."

"What about the river option?" I asked.

"As much as I want that to happen and as much as it seems like the logical option, it won't work for all the same reasons as before. The river is way too swollen and the channels are too fast. Even in the best of boats we'd be challenged to make it anywhere close to a town with an airport. Plus we'd be tossed and turned all the way down and the Buckley's boat is not built for what's happening in that river right now. You think the ATV ride over here was bad – the river would be ten times worse. Mom would never make it."

"Is there anything else I missed?" I asked.

"When you live in rural Alaska your basic modes of transportation in the summer are water or air or on foot, and walking isn't realistic with the bogs in the tundra. Besides, Mom couldn't walk far enough and we couldn't carry her far enough. If it were winter, we could use a snow machine on the frozen rivers and be out in no time, but in summer and early fall, it boils down to water or air. Unfortunately."

"Okay. Then let's batten down the hatches. Let's get in as secure a location in this house as possible and wait out this weather. I also think we should expect visitors sometime before morning and we better be prepared."

"Prepared how?" she asked.

"I have no idea. But let's start the process and see what happens. It's only two-thirty now so we have a lot of sunlight left—which in this case is a bad thing. We need to make the kitchen look like it hasn't been used in a couple of months, and we can't use light unless the room has no windows. We need to move your Mom to the most secure location. Let's look for the safest spot in the house before she wakes up so when she does, we can give her some food and pills and keep her comfortable before she nods off again. I'll play lookout. "

India went about returning the kitchen to the condition we found it in while I checked out the house. There were three bedrooms but all of them had windows with old blinds that weren't secure. There was a small sleeping loft that looked over the family room where Helen was sleeping now. It had no window but might be a good spot for me to use as a lookout but it would be tough to hide in if someone came into the house.

The hallway between the kitchen and the back bedrooms had a long narrow carpet runner. I picked it up and found a trap door beneath. I pulled open the door and saw a set of concrete stairs that led to a basement. There was a light switch on the wall inside the trap door. I switched it on and lowered myself down into the opening and onto the first concrete stair. I went down the remaining six steps and entered a half-basement under the kitchen. It had the hot water heater, an old furnace that by the look of it hadn't been used in some time, and a water pump, presumably for pumping water from the well into the house. The basement also had racks of tools and household gadgets that clearly hadn't been used in years, plus two chairs and an old version of a LazyBoy recliner. This could be perfect.

I called up to India. She came over to the opening and looked down at me.

"Oh my God!"

"Yeah. I have a cabin in the Adirondack mountains that was built in the 1930s and it has the same feature. A half-basement accessed through a trapdoor located in the dining room hallway. Who in the hell would have thought?"

"Holy shit!" she said, lowering herself through the opening. "I can't believe this. Will it work?"

"I can't think of a better hiding place. We all walked over that trapdoor a dozen times and never knew it was there. This could be our ticket, or at least as good as it'll get for us."

"How are we going to get Mom down here?"

"Super carefully. There's a small stepstool in the back bedroom and I think I can use that to help her step down onto the top cement step, so we won't have to lower her through the opening, which would be impossible. Let's get some provisions down here, lights and anything else we might need tonight, and then we'll see what the rest of the afternoon brings. I'll set up the stool and we'll have a game plan in case something crazy happens."

India and I spent the next thirty minutes stocking the basement with food, water, lights, and plenty of blankets, and situating the recliner for maximum comfort for Helen. I put the stepstool on the first basement step and hoped Helen could make it down if I held her from the bottom while India helped from above. The one thing we couldn't account for was bathroom facilities, so we took down an old pot we found under the kitchen sink.

Back in the living room, Helen was still asleep. It was three-thirty. A lot of afternoon left. We needed to lay low and focus on keeping her comfortable, while staying inside the house. India and I took a nap in the back bedroom while Helen rested in the living room.

At five o'clock I awoke with a start to the sound of a roar outside the house. India and I both jumped out of bed. We moved through the house, crouching to avoid being seen through the windows. I went into the living room where Helen was still sleeping and looked out the front windows toward the river. As if on cue, a sea plane roared past the front windows not more than 50 feet in the air. The whole house shuddered as the plane banked over the house. I crouched down beneath the window sash and looked out. The plane banked sharply to the right, then flew a straight course away from the house for a quarter mile, then banked sharply again and headed back. I could see its wings bucking and turning in the turbulent air and the plane itself jerked from side to side almost nonstop. Someone was crazy enough to fly in these conditions and this close to the house—someone who was outraged. It was easy to know who that was. As far as I could tell there was at least one other person in the plane with him. India's dad must have enlisted one of his crazy friends to help him—I was pretty sure that wasn't Jacob in the plane; at least I hoped not.

India was sitting on the kitchen floor. Helen was trying to sit up on the couch.

"Helen, please lie back down for just a few more minutes. We have visitors," I said. Helen lay back down, her eyes open wide and a concerned look on her face.

"Here they come again," I yelled.

The plane came closer this time, seemingly just feet above the roof line. The vibration was so intense a picture fell off the living room wall. The plane pulled up sharply and banked to the left just after it passed over the house. It continued into the distance, banked again and flew down the river in the direction of India's house, bucking and lurching from side to side. We kept hidden in case binoculars were trained on us. After a few minutes there was no sound. India and I got up and silently went into the kitchen.

"At least they can fly in this weather," India whispered. "Maybe that means you can fly us out of here today? Or Caleb can make it in?"

"Let's remember my skill set. In perfect conditions I might be able to make it to Anchorage but add one or two elements reducing perfect conditions and you increase the risk exponentially. High winds are one of the worst things for an amateur pilot to navigate."

"What about Caleb?"

"You forgot—I don't have the phone to call Caleb. Jacob was supposed to bring it and he never showed up. He might have called Caleb himself from the house but there's no way for us to know that or get a message to Caleb now. Even if Caleb decided to come I doubt if he could land on the Buckleys' airstrip in this wind. That seaplane certainly couldn't land here. Your dad was just doing a reconnaissance."

India shrugged, looking uncomfortable.

"To get back to the matter at hand—I figure if your dad saw something or decides to come over here, it'll take him at least two hours. So let's get ourselves ready. Get your Mom some food and water, and then be prepared to go downstairs at around six o'clock. If they're going to come, it's likely to be before dark so we best be prepared."

"This is like a nightmare. I honestly can't believe we're doing this to avoid my dad, my own flesh and blood," she said.

"There are serious issues to be worked through after we get to Anchorage, for sure. But for now, let's just focus on keeping together and safe. The rest will come in time."

We went back to the living room and India sat on the sofa next to her mom. She stroked her hair and pulled the blankets up to her chin.

"How are you, Mom?"

"I want to go home, sweetie."

CHAPTER FOURTEEN

*"It's not what you look at that matters,
it's what you see."*

—Henry David Thoreau

We elected to go to Anchorage that day. It seemed likely that India's dad would show up, search the house, and find us, despite the trap door into the basement. Plus India's mom was getting restless and had started to complain. She wanted to go home and I couldn't blame her. This was getting difficult for her, and her husband was on our tail. India reassured her and gave her another Percocet, but we decided it would be good to get her out while we could. We had two issues – first, it was late in the day, and second, the winds were still pounding and there was occasional rain or drizzle.

It was now six. Sunset would happen at around eight-forty-five. I needed to get things in order in the hangar immediately. I figured that if India's dad had seen us from the float plane, we had inside of two hours before he showed up. Besides that, it was going to be dark soon and we absolutely had to get to Anchorage before nightfall.

I ran out the back door and over to the hanger. I opened the lock on the hangar door, then relocked it from the inside behind me. I pre-flighted the plane—I did a walk- around, checked the oil and fuel, the struts ailerons, and tires, then jumped in the plane and did all the pre-flight checks I could without the plane running. All instruments were active and the avionics were good. We were ready to load Helen and get out of here. I checked the Anchorage sectional maps again and felt reasonably confident about the general direction I needed to head. I put the Lake Hood airport into the GPS and it showed 160 miles, which would mean just slightly more than an hour-and-a-half flight from where we were. I could cruise at around 100 mph if I could get the plane off the runway.

Once the plane was ready I went back into the house, staying close to the buildings in case the float plane came back. India was waiting for me in the kitchen.

"Let's go," I said.

India's mom was still on the couch. India took her teacup, washed it out in the sink, and put it back into the cupboard. I shouldered India's backpack—India had put full water bottles on both sides. We got Helen off the couch and began moving slowly toward the door. I wasn't sure if it was the Percocet or Helen's deteriorating condition, but moving her was slower than it was earlier in the day. I looked over at India. She had a worried look on her face.

We crossed the lawn to the hangar as quickly as possible, fighting buffeting winds. Once we were inside I locked the entrance door behind us and then opened the large hangar door that opened onto the runway. We began the arduous process of getting Helen into the plane, reassuring her the whole time. Finally we got her into a comfortable position in the rear of the plane. We covered her with several layers of warm blankets and I fastened the seatbelts around her as best I could.

India got into the passenger seat and I jumped in the pilot's seat. I handed her the checklists. Pre-flight, taxi, takeoff, cruise flight and landing. We put on our headsets so we could talk to each other.

"Okay. So, these are the checklists we'll need to go through prior to take-off, during cruise and pre-landing. I need you to read each of these aloud to me at the appropriate time and I'll acknowledge the setting. After that we should be good to go."

"Okay," India replied.

We were finally ready.

I took another look at Helen. I couldn't see her face from where I was sitting, but her head was lying to the side so I assumed she was sleeping or close to it.

I turned the key and the avionics and dashboard lit up. I adjusted the throttle and mixture and turned the ignition over and the engine sprang to life.

"Okay, let's go through the taxi and pre-flight checklist," I said.

India looked over at me and began to recite the list.

"Parking brake."

"Off," I said.

"Cabin doors."

"Closed and locked."

"Seats, belts."

"Adjusted and locked"

"Flight controls."

"Free and correct."

"Instruments."

"Set."

"Fuel Quantity."

"Check."

"Fuel shutoff valve."

"Check."

"Mixture."

"Rich."

"Elevator trim."

"Set for takeoff."

We worked through the twenty-six checks for takeoff and everything was set. I checked the GPS coordinates for the Anchorage and Lake Hood landing strips and made sure they were still in the system from last night. We were ready to taxi.

"As I pull out of the hangar, look back on your side and make sure the wings are clear of the door. It should be fine but just check."

I gently gave the plane some gas and the engine roared loudly inside the hangar. I hadn't done this in at least five years. I took a deep breath. I'm not prone to being scared, but I was terrified that I was flying after a long layoff, that we were headed into horrible weather and I two lives on board that mattered to me.

We began to move slowly out into the late afternoon daylight. All the instruments were alive and everything looked perfect. We traveled over the uneven ground for a few yards, then I turned the plane to the left and began our taxi to the runway. The plane immediately started lurching from the high winds. The taxiway was rough and pitted and as we pitched back and forth to the end of the taxiway, Helen emitted a groan.

When we reached the end of the taxiway I turned right onto the runway and lined up the plane until we were headed straight down the runway. Gusts were still hammering the plane but it was shaking slightly less now as we faced directly into the wind. As strange as it seemed, I felt calm as we approached the takeoff.

We were at a full stop. We were ready to go. I looked over at India.

"Ready?" I asked.

"Yes, let's get it done. And thank you. I owe you and I'll never forget you."

I looked down at the instruments one last time, then looked up at the runway, settled into my seat, and began to apply power.

The plane nudged forward down the grass runway. As we gained speed it began to settle into a rhythmic rocking motion on the grass beneath us. At 80 miles per hour I gently pulled the yoke back and the plane softly lifted from the runway. Just as we cleared the end of the runway, I saw something move below us to my left. I looked more closely. There was someone running onto the runway. India's father had found us. India hadn't seen anything and I didn't mention that we'd been discovered. I was glad we hadn't stayed. There was no way we could have remained hidden, even given the trap door.

We safely crested the tall spruce scattered along the end of the runway like fence posts. Heavy turbulence began as soon as we crested the trees. We were slammed so hard I thought we might be tossed down into the forest beneath us. As I climbed higher the turbulence increased in intensity the higher we climbed. I kept my eyes on the GPS. Once we got to 3,000 feet, our cruise altitude, the GPS showed me our route into Anchorage and the weather ahead. The weather looked clear but I knew we'd be in heavy turbulence the entire flight as turbulence and wind aren't reflected on radar. I eased back on the throttle, set the trim, and adjusted the mixture; the cruise portion of our flight was underway. We were jerking around and the entire interior of the plane was in constant motion. Anything that wasn't held down was airborne. We were hitting pockets of turbulence so severe the cord to my headset kept hitting the roof of the plane and I would have been thrown out of my seat if not for the seatbelt.

"Okay, so that was way easier than I thought it might be," I said through the bumps.

"Yeah. But this turbulence sucks." India looked back at her mother.

"How is she?"

"Hard to believe but I think she's asleep. I gave her one and a half Percocets instead of just one. She needs whatever help she can get, and I don't think another half is going to kill her."

"Agreed."

If possible, the turbulence was getting worse. We were flying southwest toward Anchorage and the winds seemed to be coming from the northeast. So the winds were hitting us from the side and rear, affecting both the ride and the lift of the plane. It was difficult to control our altitude. I was barely able to keep the plane on a steady heading and had to increase speed slightly to counteract the drag from behind.

"I'm going to take us down to 2,000 feet to see if I can find some smoother air," I said. I pulled back slightly on the throttle which resulted in a slow reduction in airspeed and altitude. I remembered from my flight training that power equals altitude, and as I eased the power back we began our gradual descent. As we moved towards 2,500 feet, the plane did a violent lurch. I held the yoke firmly. India and I had both been yanked up against our seat belts again. We looked back. Helen was awake and moaning, her eyes alive with fear. She had been tossed from her makeshift bed. I could hear her cries over the plane's loud sounds as it lurched and swayed through the sky. We were being buffeted by continual gusts so severe I didn't know if I could control the plane if it got any worse.

India looked over at me.

"Is there anything you can do?

Just then we hit another big pocket. This one came from the right side and the plane began to yaw—the rear of the plane began to move to the left, toward the front of the plane. For a moment we began to move in the direction of a spin. I yanked the rudder to the right and the plane corrected. But the turbulence continued as I attempted to correct course. It was worse here than when we were at 3,000 feet.

"Hold on, we're going back up. But it's going to get worse for a few minutes because I have to increase power to get to a higher altitude. We're going to go faster momentarily as we climb. So hold on tight."

"That's impossible," India screamed.

I applied power and the plane began a gradual climb back to a higher altitude. The shaking and turbulence continued as we climbed back up to 3,000 feet. I checked the GPS: We were still over an hour out of Anchorage. I dialed up Anchorage approach on the radio to get current weather at Lake Hood. It wasn't good: high winds steady at 20 to 25 mph with gusts to 40 mph. This airplane would have a tough time landing in that. I needed to find some clear air. But moving above 3,000 feet would make us appear on Anchorage approach radar and I didn't need to interact with them just yet. I would eventually have to talk to them as I neared Anchorage but I wanted to avoid a conversation before that because they might question why I was flying a light plane in today's conditions, especially since there were airman advisories all over Alaska and they were slowing commercial traffic into Anchorage International to a crawl. It was not safe to be flying a small airplane anywhere in Alaska today.

At 3,000 feet the turbulence eased somewhat. It was still heavy, but not as bad as the constant rattling and shaking of 2,000 feet. I wanted to ease the plane up to 3,500 feet or higher just to see. We were still close to eighty miles out from Anchorage and I figured we had another half hour of flight time before we entered Anchorage control. I applied more power and we moved out of 3,000 feet to 3,500 feet, then to 3,750 feet. I stopped the climb. There was still heavy turbulence at 3,750 feet but it was slightly better than at any other altitude. Or maybe I was wishing that was the case or maybe we were just getting used to it.

We were flying between two levels of clouds. The ones below us was my concern because as a VFR pilot I was not qualified to fly in clouds. The clouds below us were sparse but I kept a constant watch on them in case they got thicker. If they did I would need to descend through them into clear air, which would mean more turbulence. I made sure I could always spot the ground, even though through the translucent clouds. My biggest fear with the clouds other than seeing through them was the possibility of icing on the wings. That would be the end of us.

We held our position at 3,750 feet. The turbulence began to moderate a little, becoming constant moderate buffeting punctuated by moments of severe jerking, as opposed to a constant state of battering and pummeling like we had earlier. I took a breath and drank some water.

"How is she?" I asked. I had been concentrating so intently on flying I hadn't looked back at Helen in some time.

"Who knows. It looks like she's in and out of consciousness. At the moment she's sleeping."

"In ten minutes we'll enter Anchorage airspace and I'll need to talk to them. I'm going down below 3,000 feet so I stay away from TRACON but I'll still have to talk to the tower. I'm trying to fly below the radar, literally. At about that same time we'll begin our descent, which means we'll get cell service. You should get on the phone and see about arranging an ambulance to meet us. When we get lower it will also get really bumpy again, so prepare for that."

"Okay. Mom's lying on her side and I can't see her face. If we have ten minutes, I think I'll climb back there and check on her before we land."

"Be careful. It's still really bad. You should be fastened in. We only have a few minutes before we start our descent and you can't be back there not buckled in."

"I'll be quick."

She unbuckled her seat belt, moved her seat as far forward as she could to create an alleyway between the front and rear portions of the plane, and crawled into the back.

I kept our altitude steady and looked at the GPS again. Seventy-five miles to Anchorage. We were getting close.

It was 7:15 p.m. We would get to Anchorage before dark, which was critical. The clouds up ahead were taking on a soft orange color as the sun began to drop ever so slightly into the western sky. Had it not been for our circumstances, I would have marveled at the beautiful sky around us. Off in the distance, I could just barely see lights from the far eastern hamlets outside of Anchorage. We were approaching Cook Inlet and I could see where the great tidal flats met the massive peaks of the Chugach mountains, which rise from the Pacific just outside Anchorage. It was stunning. For a moment we seemed to be suspended in place—the turbulence had died down and we were bathed in a cocoon of beauty.

I looked at the GPS again. We were fifty miles out. I looked back at India. She was lying beside her mother, stroking her hair. She didn't look up at me.

I reduced power to start our descent. As soon the plane slowed and began its descent the severe turbulence began again. I quickly looked back and motioned India to take her seat. She climbed up through the alley between the seats, fastened in, and put her headphones on.

"How is she?"

"She's alive but drugged up, which is good. Her breathing seems a bit shallow but maybe that's just because of the drugs and the drama. I really don't know."

"We're almost there. We'll be down in twenty minutes. Why don't we do a landing checklist now that you're back. We're still a bit high for that but I think it's going to get very bumpy and I'd just a soon get the checklist over with so I can hang onto the yoke and try to keep us centered."

India got out the checklist.

"Fuel Selector."

"On"

"Mixture."

"Rich."

"Carb Heat."

"On."

"Seatbelts."

"Fastened."

"Flight instruments."

"Checked and set."

"Radios."

"Checked."

"ATIS."

"Checked."

"Landing lights"

"On."

We were descending through 2,750 feet and severe turbulence was once again upon us. We were bouncing from one pocket to another, and in between the plane never stopped shaking. We were in constant motion, both vertically and horizontally, and it was all I could do to keep the plane on a straight heading into Anchorage. I was also having trouble keeping the engine at a steady speed because each time we were thrown the wind hit the prop and affected the engine timing. There was absolutely nothing I could do to calm the ride. Despite the chaos, the view around us was spectacular. It was oxymoronic – I was terrified about keeping the plane in the air while we were surrounded by the most beautiful vistas imaginable. We could see the entire length of the Cook Inlet as well as Anchorage sitting at the base of the mountains just feet from the ocean. We were heading directly toward downtown Anchorage. When we were five miles out I would make a sweeping left turn, then swing back right and head back toward the inlet and Lake Hood as we lined up for landing.

When we hit 2,500 feet, I radioed control. We were cleared direct to Lake Hood and there were no comments about our choice of days to fly. I looked over. India was searching her phone.

"I think you should call an ambulance," I said. "We'll be landing in ten minutes and we'll park at Dorsey's Air Service. I'll radio them now and make sure they have a parking space for us. Also don't forget to call the Buckleys. I don't have a clue how you're going to handle this with them." She stopped typing on her phone and looked over at me.

"Now's not the time for that."

I radioed Dorsey's and got clearance for a parking spot close to the terminal. They didn't ask any questions and I didn't offer. I told them we would be parked for five days, which I figured would be enough time for India to figure out how to get the plane back to the Buckleys' camp. We were in uncharted territory—flying an airplane that wasn't ours, running from India's crazed father, transporting a very sick woman. And to top it off, I was flying without a license. The only light at the end of the tunnel was that we were now turning on our final approach and in a few minutes this chapter would be over.

The lower we got the rougher the turbulence was. We were now on a three-mile final and the plane was being thrown around so hard that it was close to impossible, with reduced power, to keep it lined up with the Lake Hood glide path. I feared I would go into a stall because I couldn't control altitude or power. There were nearly constant warning chimes coming from the avionics as I struggled to keep the plane's bearing consistent. Each time we hit an air pocket it took forever to correct the heading into Lake Hood and we were running out of time to get lined up correctly. The nose of the plane was being thrown from side to side and I lost track of the runway every time we were tossed to the side. The only alternative to landing at Lake Hood was Anchorage International, which sits just west of Lake Hood. But the controllers would not take kindly to a Cessna landing on their runways, and there was no place to park once I was there. Plus, at the least I would get fined for landing if not arrested for flying without a license. I had to make Lake Hood happen. India was holding onto her seat bottom and a metal grab bar above her, in order to stay in her seat. I took a quick look back and saw Helen being thrown from side to side and up and down. She looked like a rag doll but she wasn't making any noise that I could hear. I hoped she was still alive.

As we got closer to the field I kept our landing power as high as possible to avoid any abrupt drops, which could cause a crash. We crossed the lake and came over the landing strip and I pushed the nose down. Just before it hit I flared the front, cut power and settled the tires onto the dirt runway. The plane bounced two or three times violently, the wings caught wind gusts which lifted the nose back off the runway twice, but I was able to settle the plane down, manage braking and quickly we were in taxi mode. We had made it.

"Holy shit," I said.

"Oh my God. That was insane. There's no way we should have made it," India said. "I've never experienced anything like that in my entire life. Damn."

"We're here – we made it." I looked over at India as we began the taxi and the look of relief on her face was palpable. She looked better than she had since Caleb had flown out to the spring creek to break the news three days prior. I couldn't have had a better partner for the chaos we were engulfed in and I already knew I didn't want to ever let her go.

"Let's swing into action," I said.

"The ambulance should be here or close. I called them as soon as I got cell reception," she said.

As we made the short taxi to Dorsey's, India released her seat belt, pushed the seat forward, and once again climbed into the back with her mother. I could see her crawling over the blankets to come up beside her mom, lowering her head to speak to her.

I pulled the plane up to the terminal area at Dorsey's and a member of their ground crew came out to guide me in. Once settled, I shut off the engine while the ground crew put chocks on the wheels. I opened the door.

"You're either the most daring pilot on earth, with balls of steel, or the dumbest bastard I've ever seen," the ground crew member said.

"It would be the latter. But we had to fly today. We have a very sick passenger with us."

"I heard. Well, welcome to Anchorage—sometime when you get a minute I'd like to hear about that flight. Never seen a 172 fly in those conditions, let alone make it. Cheers to you."

I got out of the plane and moved the front seat forward as far as it would go. India and her mom were still huddled together in the rear of the plane.

"How are things?" I asked.

"We're good. Just relaxing a bit before we get out," India said.

"Okay. I'm going to go talk to the office about leaving the plane here and find out where the ambulance is. Be right back."

The terminal was little more than a metal pole building with a reception desk, a very small seating area with a coffee pot in the corner, and a view onto both the dirt runway and the Lake Hood seaplane runway. There was one man standing at the check-in counter watching me approach.

"I just came in with the Cessna. We're going to need to park the plane here for a few days."

"How long exactly?" he asked.

"Let's say five days." "Someone will be back to get it no later than that and probably sooner, but I'm not sure. My priority now is to get a sick person to the hospital."

"How do you want to pay for the parking and service?" he asked.

"How much is it?"

"$125 a day for tie-down plus whatever fuel you need."

I passed my credit card over the desk and he processed it while looking at me.

"That your plane?" he asked.

"No. It's a longer story than I have time to tell you but no. It's not mine. A friend loaned it to us." I signed the receipt. As I turned to go back outside, I saw the ambulance driving down the access road to the front of the terminal. I could also see India and her mom sitting up in the back of the plane. Both were good news. I ran out to the plane.

"We're set with parking," I told India. "How's it going?"

"We're doing all right."

"Hi, Helen. How are you feeling?"

"I'm not feeling well. But thanks for working this hard to get me here." She said the words with some difficulty, her voice barely audible.

I got back into the terminal just as the EMTs were arriving, stretcher in tow. I introduced myself.

"Hi, I'm Eli—we're the ones who called you."

"This is a transport to Alaska Regional, right?"

"Right."

"And the patient has a broken shoulder and possibly a stroke?"

"Correct."

"When did both happen?"

"Four days ago."

They looked at each other and then back at me.

"It's a long story," I said. "But we couldn't get her out any earlier. And frankly, it wasn't a good idea to fly here today, but it is what it is. Let's go get her—she's in a Cessna out back and it'll take some maneuvering to get her out." I said as I turned to walk back through the terminal building and out the back door with the EMT's behind me.

We got to the plane and they readied the stretcher. The wind was still howling around us and there was no activity on the field. I climbed into the cramped space in the back of the plane. Helen looked terrible, ashen faced and tiny, curled up into India with blankets covering her.

"Okay Helen. We need to move you closer to the door so the EMTs can get you onto the stretcher. Can you use your good arm to help us slide you this way?" I asked.

She nodded and India began to help her slide slowly toward the door. It was difficult and painful for Helen because she could only use her good arm to support herself. She got closer to the door and it was time for her to lay down so we could lift her out.

"Let us take it from here, sir," one of the EMTs said from behind me. I moved to the side and they pulled Helen closer to the door and moved the stretcher in position just outside the plane. They pulled a large back brace out from under the stretcher.

"Ma'am, my name is Jason and Corey here and I are going to get you to the hospital. How are you doing right now?"

Helen looked up at them and smiled. "I'm okay."

"Great. I'm going to pull you just a little further toward the door, then we're going to slide this long board under you so we can lift you onto the stretcher. The board may be a little hard to get under you, but once we do you'll feel much less pain getting onto the stretcher. Does that sound good?"

"Yes."

The two EMTs pulled Helen as close to the door as possible, then skillfully maneuvered the board under her by rocking her very gently from side to side. Once it was in place, they secured her with belts and lifted her onto the stretcher. They covered her with blankets, then moved her toward the terminal and the ambulance waiting in the parking lot.

India got out of the plane. I grabbed my backpack and slammed the door shut and we followed the stretcher. I was unsure what was going to happen next. We hadn't discussed what was in store once we got here. India turned to me as we entered the terminal building and put her hand on my arm.

"Come with us to the hospital," she said. "I have no idea what your plans are now that we're here, but please come with us so we can talk once we get her settled."

"Okay."

CHAPTER FIFTEEN

"When you are sorrowful look again in your heart, and you shall see in truth that you are weeping for that which has been your delight."

—Kahlil Gibran

India and I sat at a sterile Formica table in the stale hospital cafeteria with its pastel walls and the ever-present smell of antiseptic. We had cups of lukewarm coffee in Styrofoam cups that we were fidgeting with, plus one blueberry muffin from a vending machine. Its wrapper was lying open on the table, with crumbs spread around the crumbled pieces that we had messed with.

Finally India broke the silence. "I don't know how to thank you for everything you've done," she said, her head lowered, looking down at the table.

"Please stop thanking me. It's nothing you wouldn't have done for me."

"It's just that in spite of how hard things have been these past few days, now comes the hardest part."

I knew what she was talking about but I had to ask. "What do you mean?"

"I mean we've been so focused on getting Mom here through all kinds of adversity that we haven't thought about what happens next with the two of us. Now that we're here I want to talk about that, and also how you're leaving soon. We never got to talk about what comes next."

She looked up at me.

"Yeah, you're right. We've talked about everything but us," I said. "We've been through a war, but we didn't talk about what happens when we achieve peace."

She reached across the table and took both my hands.

"I spoke with Jacob while I was with Mom upstairs. He said it's been pure hell at the house since we left. Dad came back while he was trying to call Caleb and when he found out we'd left, he went nuts and accused both Jacob and Ruth of being involved and threatened them both. Eventually then pled ignorance and he turned his attention to you and me, but anyway, they're coming in. He, Ruth and Dad will be here tomorrow. There's nothing Dad can do now. Mom's had emergency surgery on her shoulder and by the time they get here she'll be resting. The doctors have already started her stroke protocol. He lost the battle, but the war's just begun. It'll be a bitch, but we did the right thing. I've been thinking. It's hard to say this after everything you've done to get Mom here, but I don't think you should be here when they arrive. I want you to be here more than anything, believe me, but I don't think it helps our cause. We need to move through this as a family, and your presence is a lightning rod for him. I hope you understand."

"I do."

"Look, Mom's out of surgery but won't be fully wake and functional until sometime early tomorrow because they want to keep her sedated so she'll be out of it all night, so why don't we get a room, have some dinner, and make as nice an evening for ourselves as we can," she said. "They'll call me if Mom wakes up or if there are any issues. If I need to get over here I can."

"That sounds good. I already got a room at the Captain Cook so we're set."

"Thank you. I'm going to speak with the doctor one last time and let them know our plan. Why don't you go over to the hotel and freshen up, and I'll call you when I'm on the way."

"Okay," I said. I pushed back my chair, grabbed my backpack, wrapped up the muffin crumbs, and turned to head out. I kissed her lightly on the cheek before I left the room.

The Captain Cook Hotel is the grand dame of Anchorage hotels. Sitting on a rise overlooking downtown Anchorage, it has played host to groups of international dignitaries, politicians, Presidents, and luminaries from across the globe for more than fifty years, and its three towers are an iconic symbol of both Anchorage and Alaska. Most of the guest rooms overlook Cook Inlet and the mountains to the south. Their vast panoramic views bring home the majesty that is Alaska to visitors from across the globe.

I got a suite on the top floor and spoke to my office in New York. Then I booked myself on a flight back to New York via Seattle at 3:40 p.m. the following day.

I ordered two vintage bottles of wine from room service and poured myself a drink from the hotel mini bar. I looked out over downtown Anchorage and at the Chugach Mountains and the Cook Inlet, where I had just come from. It was evening now and just a few rays of light persisted over the horizon. The rain was gone but the wind was still heavy. I could hear it as it lashed the hotel windows. It looked like they had resumed flight operations at Anchorage International. What a day.

My cell phone rang. It was India.

"Hey."

"Hey. Everything's more or less good with Mom. She's dehydrated, has a shoulder that's broken in numerous places and is now held together with plates and screws. She did have a stroke, but thankfully it was mild. They expect a full recovery on all fronts, but the rehab will take months. They suggest she stay in Anchorage for both rehab protocols."

"Just as you thought, then," I said.

"More or less, yeah. Again, it was the right thing to do. To bring her here. Even with all the nonsense and drama, it was critical and probably life-saving to do what we did.

"Anyway, I'm on my way. What's the room number?"

"842. See you in a couple of minutes."

India showed up looking beat and her clothes were a rumpled mess. I had stopped in a shop in the lobby and purchased a pair of jeans and a new shirt along with some toiletries. All my luggage was still at India's house in the bush. It didn't matter that I probably wouldn't see any of it again.

"How about we go downstairs and get you some new clothes and whatever toiletries you need?" I suggested. "Then we can clean up and have some dinner."

"Does your fancy suite have robes?"

"Yes, it does."

She walked over to me and put her arms around my waist. "How about we take a shower, together, get into those robes and have dinner at that table right over there overlooking the most beautiful scenery imaginable until we are too tired and too drunk to do anything but sleep all of this chaos off for a night? I'm just not sure we need any clothes."

"Deal."

I rolled over and looked at the clock. It was 7:00 a.m. The last thing we discussed before the wine took over was that we should be up by nine. Jacob had texted her and said they planned to be in town by noon. She needed to check on her mom no later than mid-morning.

I looked around and saw that the room was a mess. What was left of the food and three empty wine bottles crowded the dirty table, and our clothes were strewn everywhere. The robes were nowhere in sight. I could see the sun coming up through a crease in the blinds. India was still fast asleep and sprawled across the bed.

I crept out of bed as carefully and quietly as possible, walked into the outer room of the suite, and closed the door behind me. I found a robe, put it on, and tied it around my waist. Luckily, there was a coffee maker in the outer room and I started a brew. My computer and cell phone were set up at a desk.

I booted up my computer and started going through the laundry list of issues and problems at my office. My car was confirmed to pick me up at the hotel at 2:00 p.m. It was set—I was leaving today.

I leaned back in my chair with my coffee and looked out over the Alaskan landscape that I had come to love so much. A few minutes later cool hands made their way inside my robe and started massaging my neck.

"Oh, so nice, thank you," I said. "Just what the doctor ordered after three bottles of wine last night."

"Plus, two shots and then two hours of rolling around on our king-sized bed."

"Oh yeah, I forgot about that."

She swatted the back of my head.

"Let's sit. I'll get you a cup of coffee, and I ordered room service. It should be here shortly," I said.

She sat on the sofa, crossed her legs, and brought the length of her hair around to the front of her robe. I moved over next to her. She finally looked at me.

"Not to be a buzzkill on this beautiful morning," I said, "but I've got a flight later this afternoon."

I heard her draw a quick breath. "Oh my God." I looked at her and saw tears in her eyes. She set her coffee cup on the table. I moved closer and grabbed her hand.

"Look, this isn't the end of our relationship."

She was quiet, still not looking at me.

"I have an idea. I have a house in Telluride, Colorado. I think I may have mentioned that. Let's meet there in a couple weeks. There will be no distractions. Just you and me. We can fish and hike and I'll show you country as beautiful and wild as this. Everything with your parents will be behind us then. And then we'll see."

"I don't know, honestly. I'm horrified by the idea of never seeing you again. But at the same time, it's complicated. I'm supposed to leave for Mexico with my sister in a couple of weeks and we've been planning that trip for months."

There was a knock at the door and I got up to answer it. Room service. We moved over to the table by the window and I uncovered our breakfast and poured more coffee, then sat down. She was silent and her eyes were still wet with tears. We had only an hour together before she had to leave.

She sat with her legs crossed at an angle to the table, so she was facing the window instead of me. She stared out at the view.

"Hey," I said.

She looked at me.

"We can sort this out over the coming days. You have other fish to fry now, so let's not pile on. I'm sorry."

"It's okay. Just a lot to think about," she said. "But—I want you to know I'll never forget you and I'll never forget this week. Both the good and the bad. It was amazing to have you in my life this week and I couldn't have done it without you."

She got up and came around the table and kissed me.

"Now I have to take a long shower. It's getting late and I'll be getting a text sooner rather than later."

We were quiet during the elevator ride to the lobby. I have a hard time remembering every moment of it. I think that's generally true with traumatic moments in our lives. I just remember that I wasn't leaving until later in the day, so we only had her backpack with us. We held hands like we'd been holding hands for years. She'd gotten the text and was meeting her family at the hospital at eleven a.m. It was now ten-thirty. We were leaving later than we had planned but we'd needed to make love one more time.

We got off the elevator, walked through the lobby and over to the entrance, and emerged into a brilliant, windless morning just as her Uber pulled up to the entrance. We held each other closely.

"This feels like love to me," I said. "I don't want to ever let you go."

"I know. I feel the same."

When she looked up at me I saw that her eyes were filled with tears. The Uber driver waited and the bellmen stood patiently to the side as we kissed under the entrance canopy. Then India got into the Uber and slammed the door and the car drove away.

TELLURIDE

Flying into Telluride is never easy, especially when you're coming from Alaska. She was on a Delta flight from Anchorage via Salt Lake City into Grand Junction. I waited in the terminal building for her. A large group of smoke jumpers were sleeping or texting on their phones along the back wall, presumably catching some downtime before their last deployment to a fire outside of Dolores, Colorado, or at least I was guessing that was where they were headed. They looked dirty, tired and beat up.

I had spoken to India three or four times since we parted in Anchorage. I had been back in New York resuming my life as best I could, and she was still dealing with family issues. Her dad went ballistic when he got to Anchorage, but the police handled that. Her mom was recovering nicely, walking on a treadmill and gaining weight, spending most of her days outside her rehab unit. She was in good spirits and healing. Ruth and Jacob were still in a state of shock from the ordeal, as was India, I suspected, but she said she was fine. There seemed to be a distance in our conversations but maybe that was my imagination. She was a woman of few words anyway and on the phone she was even quieter. The physical distance didn't help. I'd soon find out. She was on her way.

I went to the airport restaurant and got a coffee, then walked over and sat in a chair near her gate and overlooking the one runway. The Grand Junction airport is so small you can sit outside security and still be only a few steps away from the gates. I was just a few yards from where she would disembark. There was very little activity in or outside the airport, except for the smoke jumpers' planes which were being refueled in a parking area off to the side. In a little deli that sat close to security the attendant was reading a book and country music was playing. It was a quiet day in Grand Junction.

It was also a beautiful sunny day with an expected high in the low seventies. The forecast for our weekend was perfect. Beautiful blue skies, abundant sunshine, little chance of rain and warm, early fall days.

I sat in the chair with my coffee for maybe a half hour, looking out the long plate glass windows that ringed the departures area of the airport. Then I saw her plane approaching from the west, a dot way off in the distance but approaching quickly, winding its way through the high valleys that ringed the airport, finally making a wide downwind turn, then lining up with the runway on final approach. She was here.

The plane landed, taxied to the gate, and shut down its engines. The gate agent opened the door leading to the jetway and walked down to open the airplane door, and a few minutes later passengers started walking off. She appeared through the jetway door and looked around for me. I was standing just off to the side, waiting for her. She was her typical self. Jeans, a blue pearl-snap shirt, baseball cap, flip flops, her long hair in a French braid. She looked tan and healthy. She looked over at me and smiled. I walked over to the edge of security. When I first saw her I thought about her saying "It's complicated" back in Anchorage, and when I remembered Ruth saying India was complicated and things never worked out between her and boyfriends, but that if there was ever a match for her it was me - my heart seized and I was ecstatic she was here. And then there was that smile and as she came closer both of us gained momentum until I reached her and hugged her tightly, kissed her and picked her up off her feet and swung her around and I could feel our happiness.

"Dude, I can't believe I'm here! It's so freakin' nice to see you." She said as we were pulling out of the airport in the old Jeep that I kept in Telluride, a beer already in her hand from the cooler I'd brought with me. She was leaning across the center console with her hand resting on my arm as I drove.

"No shit," I said. "You're beautiful. Thanks for coming."

"Oh please. I couldn't turn down this offer," she said with a smile.

We wound our way out of Grand Junction and got on highway 50, passed the Dominguez-Escalante National Conservation area and headed to Nucla, then to Olathe, Montrose, Ridgeway and finally up route 145 into Telluride.

The area between Grand Junction and Telluride sits on the western slope of the Colorado Rockies, well west of the continental divide, where the Rockies gradually slope down to meet the flat ranch land of extreme western Colorado and eastern Utah. The western slope still retains much of its native, undeveloped look from generations ago—broad high desert plains punctuated by deep canyons alongside the Uncompaghre Plateau and the Gunnison River. At Montrose you begin to see the outlines of the high peaks of the San Juan mountains, their tops soaring over the landscape as you approach Ridgeway, and once you turn onto 145 at Placerville, you begin a sixteen-mile climb up to Telluride, past iconic Mt. Wilson and into the famous box canyon where Telluride is housed, ringed by 13,000 foot mountains.

We all have indifferent spaces in our hearts and minds, but when one is in Telluride, it's hard to be indifferent about much. Here, the soaring spires of the San Juan range rise like statues from the mountain floor. Telluride's Main Street sits at 8,750 feet, making it the fifth highest city in the US, and the peaks that surround the town are all at or above 13,000 feet. It's commonly referred to as *little Switzerland*. The town itself sits in the back of a box canyon, nestled in a spherical cocoon of mountains like a baby in a blanket. It has only one road into town and with a population of around 2,000 permanent residents, it's a place uniquely itself.

All of that, combined with the fact that the town sits in portions of both the San Juan National Forest and the Uncompahgre National Forest with one of the finest, most magnificent freestone rivers running through it, and you have paradise on earth.

During the trip from Grand Junction to Telluride we had the windows rolled down and were drinking beer, laughing, listening to music and talking nonstop. The trip flew by. When we finally pulled into the driveway of my old Victorian house on West Columbia Avenue, India looked up at the house and said, "Oh my God! This is yours?"

"Yup. Let's go have a look and get unpacked."

I parked the Jeep and unloaded her backpack and the cooler. She had brought a large backpack and a small hand-carried bag. I lifted the backpack onto my shoulders and turned to walk with her up the few steps to the door.

I opened the door and she walked into the foyer. I leaned her pack against the entry wall and switched on a table lamp next to the door. She stood still beside me, looking around the living room just off to our left and the dining room to our right, both still wallpapered in original turn-of-the-century wallpaper. The sun poured through the windows casting shadows on the sparse mix of vintage and contemporary furniture in both rooms and on the curved walnut bannister on the stairs in front of us.

Some years prior, I had purchased this house, a large period Victorian home nestled in a historic area of town that was filled with these breathtaking homes that Telluride is known for. Most of the houses around it were much larger than mine, but this house was my escape, my relief valve, my Shangri-La, filled with century-old character and charm. Its creaky wood floors, floor-to-ceiling full leaded windows, curved walnut bannister, and original pounded tin ceilings provided me with a refuge that is hard to describe. Generations of residents had lived here before me dating back more than a century, and I found comfort in my sense of their history etched in the walls of my house.

Telluride was originally inhabited by the Ute Indians as a summer camp and named by Spanish explorers in the 1700's. I figured my house probably dated back to the early 1880s. It was still mostly original, and the first-floor rooms and kitchen ceiling were fifteen feet high. On summer mornings, with the doors and windows open and the coffee brewing on the stove, I could smell the lilacs in the backyard. At night families of coyotes walked down Liberty Bell and Tomboy Road, passing just a few blocks behind the house. I heard their howls at night as I lay in bed.

"It's breathtaking," India said softly. "More than breathtaking. It's perfect. I had no idea what to expect but it wasn't this." She turned and smiled up at me, her graceful eyes illuminated by the sun drenching the room.

"Thanks. I've worked hard to honor the house's bones. I've always felt it deserved to be left somewhat in its original condition, with only a few necessary updates here and there to help her make it through the years. Things like a new roof, some work to the fireplace. But mostly I thought it would be more authentic, more Telluride, more me, if I left it in its original form or as close to it as I can keep it."

As we stood in the foyer, we were disturbed by a loud noise, then some ruckus down the hall, and my lab Otter came shooting around a corner and sprinted over to us. She wasn't shy and went right for India, dancing a circle around her, wagging her tail and doing everything she could to get attention and affection. India knelt and let Otter have all of her – sloppy licks and squeals of happiness from both of them.

"It just keeps getting better," she said laughing and looking up at me, Otter still licking her from head to toe. "What's her name?"

"Otter. The fall is a fairly quiet time at work, so I get extended periods here and she always comes out with me."

"You drive from New York?"

"Yeah, but I've got family in Iowa, so the drive isn't a total loss. Even so, the drive isn't something I look forward to. If I need to go back to New York for a brief period, I can fly and leave her here with friends and she's happy as a clam. But then again, she's always as happy as a clam."

"Let me show you around," I said.

We turned right and walked through the simple period dining room with its long Shaker dining table and chairs and built-in hutch in the corner that was original to the house. Then we went into the kitchen with its soaring ceiling, huge Chambers Imperial gas stove that dated back to the late '20s or early '30s, and whitewashed aspen cabinets. India followed me as I circled back into the living room. The living room had original hard wood floors, an intricate woven rug that I got in China filled almost the entire long room, with a small period upholstered loveseat and sofa and side chair, two floor lamps, and a table lamp on a small end table between the sofa and loveseat, all in front of a fireplace that occupied one entire wall of the room. Otter followed us wherever we went.

I gathered India's gear and walked upstairs to the second floor. The house has three bedrooms, all on the second floor. Since it's a period house they're all small. The master is indistinguishable from the others, but it's closest to the full bath that I partially updated with a claw foot tub and black-and-white subway tile floor and walls. The one distinguishable feature of the master bedroom is that it sits on the rear corner of the house so the floor-to-ceiling lead windows run the entire length of two walls.

I put India's backpack on the ottoman at the foot of the master bed. It was a beautiful breezy day. The windows were open, and the breeze was softly blowing the window sheers. They billowed a few feet into the room with each breeze. The air smelled of early fall, a combination of warmth and coolness carried on the breeze with the smell of aspen leaves and pines just feet outside the windows.

"Are you tired?" I asked.

"A little. I don't want to sleep though. I want to stay awake so I don't lose any time here. This is too perfect, too beautiful. I'm just so struck by how beautiful your house and this town is. Honestly, I had no idea. Its paradise."

I reached out to her, I kicked off my shoes and lay back on the bed. The bed has a custom feather topper, so it's akin to sleeping in a nest. She lay down beside me and cooed a relaxing *"oh"* as her shoulders settled into the feathers. I reached down and slipped off her flip-flops just as another breeze blew in. Her feet were hot. She had her head propped up on the feather pillow and was watching me. Otter was lying beside the bed in her dog bed, licking her paws and looking up at us. Everyone and everything was content. At least for this moment, we didn't have a care in the world. Cares might come later, I reminded myself. Later I was going to have to ask her what was happening between us. But for now I was content.

We settled deeper into the bed, lying on our backs looking up at the ceiling dating back 150 years ago. The ceiling had smoke stains from a fireplace that had once been in the room, and the walls were oiled with over a century of people's movements and conversations and whispers safely sealed in its cracks. I took a breath and smelled the house's smell, a sort of tannin that hung in the air and brought back memories of wood smoke, mountain air, and moisture that only the high alpine mountains can bring. Every room in this house had a story, but I liked the stories in this room the best. I always imagined the sights and sounds that the house must have witnessed over the century. Tales of success and failure, heartache and happiness and everything in-between.

India and I were quiet and held hands and within a few minutes she was fast asleep, her grip on my hand relaxing as she fell deeper into sleep. We had been talking when she began to slowly doze off and I turned my head and watched her breathe, her mouth slightly open and her chest rising and falling. She had been up for nearly 24 hours traveling here from Alaska. For me, it was nice to be close to her after not seeing her for a month and not knowing if I would see her again. The intimacy of just lying beside her was comforting. After a few minutes I too lay back on the pillow and fell immediately asleep.

I awoke first, after about 45 minutes. India was still sleeping. I slid my arm out from under her neck, quietly swung my legs over the edge of the bed, and walked out into the hallway, Otter following me. Old houses tend to be creaky, and this one was more so than any old house I had ever been in. I did my best to be quiet but every footfall seemed to scream out. Still, India slept on.

I softly closed the bedroom door behind me, and Otter and I went downstairs to the kitchen. I stopped to refill her water bowl, then went out the back door onto the deck that wrapped around the side and back of the house, away from the street. I had lined the deck railing with New Guinea impatiens and they were in full bloom. I watered each of them, then sat back in a recliner and took a sip from a bottle of water I had retrieved from the fridge on the way out. Otter sat beside me as we looked up into the mountains behind the house.

It wasn't unusual to see Elk or Mountain Goats grazing on the foothills that were just a block or so from the deck. The house sat under several Aspen trees with one large Ponderosa pine that stood sentinel in the center of the backyard. It was naturally cool on the deck beneath the trees, and the breeze that lofted over us was lit with the smell of pine and aspen and if you were quiet enough, you could hear water babbling in a nearby brook that carried mountain runoff down to the San Miguel River, where we would fish over the weekend. In Telluride, everything flowed downhill.

I rose to light some candles that encircled the deck. It wasn't late enough to need them but I liked the ambiance. Otter was once again asleep on her outside bed between the back door and my chair. As I rounded the deck I heard the back door close and turned and saw India standing there. Her feet were still bare and she had changed into more comfortable clothes and looking refreshed. I thought she must have taken a quick sponge bath.

"Hey," she said

"How are you?"

"Evolving," she said. There was something in her smile as she wrapped her arms around herself and the sweater she had put on after her nap. She looked content, happy and completely relaxed. There was no tension between us not having seen each other for a month and everything seemed completely natural. "Because this is all a bit unexpected as I may have mentioned earlier," she said.

"You did say that. Unexpected in what way?"

"I just didn't think it would be this beautiful, this perfect. I'm just so struck by how beautiful your house and this town is. Honestly, I had no idea. Its paradise. When I thought about coming to Telluride and staying with you, I was thinking more ski condo, not magnificent Victorian and it's also unexpected because it tells me so much more about you and I absolutely love what I'm seeing – it's like a fairy tale, this place you've got here. I'm so grateful you're sharing it with me."

"You're my fishing buddy, who else would I share it with?"

"We hardly did any fishing. Most of the time we were running from people and flying planes without licenses and sneaking out in the middle of the night and breaking into homes and hiding."

I walked across the deck and put my arm around her waist and kissed her lightly.

"You said it wasn't breaking in."

"You know what I mean," She said, laughing and pushing me away.

"I can't think of anyone I'd rather have here, and you're the first and I hope the last person outside of Otter and me to come here. Now how about a glass of wine so we can get things started?"

"I'd love that."

I opened a bottle of deep red wine and we settled into chairs on the deck. I lit a stone firepit that was in the center of the deck and looked over at her.

"So what happened in Anchorage after I left?" I said.

"Oh yeah, that," she said. "Well, it was a complete and total shit show when Dad showed up at the hospital but I had alerted security so they were around when he arrived and I think that helped to calm him down. At that point he was okay with Ruth and Jacob so his anger was directed mostly at me, which was fine – I was over it at that point. When he heard the news about a broken shoulder and stroke, his anger was diffused somewhat and then he turned as apologetic as he can be and calmed down. The thing about a bully is that when you prove them wrong or bully them back, they quickly back down and that's what happened. He stayed in Anchorage for a few days then went back to the house where he remains."

"Jacob and Ruth have stayed on in Anchorage at my Aunt's house and they're doing fine and I think enjoying some time away from Dad and also seeing some friends.

Jacob's going home in the next week or so to help Dad prepare for winter but I think Ruth will stay in Anchorage with Mom, who is doing incredibly well by the way – you wouldn't recognize her. She's on the treadmill two hours a day, walking outside when she can, eating like a bear and going to therapy twice a week. Frankly, I haven't see her this positive and active for years."

"What will she do when the treatments are over?" I asked.

"I don't know, but I'm betting she stays in Anchorage. Her sister's there and I think she's starting to realize that Dad isn't necessarily her *better half* even though I know she still loves him. I just think they might be entering an alternative type of relationship where they commute to see each other periodically but maintain separate residences. And, frankly, I'm completely supportive of that. The woman deserves to have a normal life and by the same token, Dad also deserves what he's built, so I hope they can keep things together from a bit of a distance."

"Wow, that's big news," I said.

"Yes it is, but we're past this as a family, and I'm getting past it too, so I think it will all be fine ultimately."

"By the way, how did you break the news to the Buckley's about our hijacking their plane?"

"Luckily I have a solid relationship with them and I knew their daughter growing up, and although we weren't particularly close we were friendly. Anyway, I just do what Alaskans do – I called them, told them the entire truth, had a full service performed on the plane while it was in Anchorage, paid for all the fees obviously and then Caleb ferried the plane back out with a full tank of gas and they were happy we did what we had to do to save Mom. You know, at times like that I'm so fortunate to have grown up in the bush around people who work together. They couldn't have been more understanding."

"Damn. That's some ending to that story."

"It's not ended yet, but definitely headed in a better direction on all fronts."

I awoke at daybreak to the sound of mountain bluebirds and western tanagers singing their lilting early morning serenades outside our bedroom window. Once again it was breezy and the curtains, which had been billowing all night in the wind, continued their dance back and forth along the sills. It was cold in the room but there was bright sunshine outside. It must have gotten down into the high thirties overnight. I was naked on the bed. I had forgotten to turn the furnace on, so I quietly got out of bed and softly closed the door behind me, Otter in tow. I turned the thermostat in the upstairs hall to 72 degrees, grabbed a robe from the bathroom, and went downstairs to start the coffee and let Otter out.

The kitchen was a mess. We had clearly had fun—the three empty wine bottles were evidence. Pots and pans were strewn around the kitchen, testament to a late-night snack or maybe dinner, I couldn't recall the particulars.

I always use an old percolator when I am at the house because I like the way the smell of the brewing coffee fills the house. The aroma of arabica beans I've always found to be the perfect way to wake up in the mountains, or anywhere else for that matter.

I filled two mugs, and went back upstairs. I quietly opened the bedroom door. India was still lying in the same position. Her naked back was to me but unlike before, the quilt was covering most of the rest of her body. She must have stirred while I was gone and realized she was cold.

I set the coffee mugs on the bedside table and got back into bed.

She stirred. "Good morning. I think," she said.

I laughed.

"Good morning. I just made coffee. The kitchen and deck are a mess. We must have had one hell of a party."

"You forced me to drink. I told you I'm not a drinker, I'm an Alaskan woman used to living off the land. All this ritzy stuff is too much for me."

"Funny, it didn't seem like too much last night!"

She elbowed me and rolled onto her back, holding the covers up against her chin and inching into a seated position against the headboard.

"I need Advil."

I opened my hand holding two Advil and handed her the mug of coffee. She took the Advil and a big swig of coffee. Otter came running down the hall and leaped onto the bed.

It was still early and cold in the bedroom, as the heat had yet to find its way to our corner of the house. We sat with our backs against the headboard, covered up to our chins in a goose down comforter, our nakedness wrapped in down on top and feathers beneath us. We stayed that way until the house finally found its warmth.

We finished our coffee and finally acceded to Otter's demand to go for a hike. This morning we went up Bear Creek, which is an in-town hike that, after a couple of miles of elevation gain, dead-ends at a spectacular waterfall. Being an in-town hike there is more foot traffic than other hike options in the area, but in Telluride there is never an excess amount of people at any one location and no matter what direction you head, beauty awaits.

After taking a quick swim break in the pool below the waterfall, we decided to run back down the trail into town and by the time we got there we were relaxed and appropriately exercised. It was a spectacular morning. Bright sunshine, a very light breeze and I figured it was around 65 degrees and warming fast. On the way back, we stopped at a bakery and picked up some fresh bread for the day and each got a breakfast sandwich and coffee. We sat for a minute in the sunshine on the bakery deck, then when other dogs and people started showing up, we gathered our provisions and Otter and walked the few blocks back to the house.

"There are two things I want to show you while you're here. I mean there's a world to show you, but we only have the weekend, at least for this trip." I said. "So, the first is Gold King Basin, which is about a 25-minute drive from here to the turn off, then another hour drive into the back country where we can have dinner by one of the high alpine lakes up there. The other is Ptarmigan Lake, which is a glacial lake that sits at the top of Imogene Pass, which is about an hour drive through the rugged back country just up the road from here. That's in addition to hanging out in town and of course fishing the San Miguel, my home river."

"They all sound fantastic. I'm up for everything and don't care the order. Can we bring Otter?"

"Of course – she goes everywhere."

We threw some warm clothes in the backpack and swung by Smith's Market to pick up some provisions, soft drinks and beer on our way to Gold King Basin. We spent the entire day and early evening up in the basin watching Elk and Mountain Goats play along the base of the 14,000-foot peaks that rimmed the basin; elk in the lower portion eating the grass that grew alongside the two lakes that sat at the bottom and the Goats scattering along the rocks well up into the peaks.

There's an old mining road that runs through the basin that was used by prospectors back in the 1800's. The road, or what is left of it, starts at the bottom and runs up the sides of the mountains in a series of switchbacks, until it gets to the rock outcroppings at the base of the cliffs where it becomes too steep to drive and where most of the abandoned mines are located. As you drive up the road, you pass deserted mine entrances, their tailings evidence of where the shaft had been. The basin is several miles wide, so the expanse is dramatic. We had the entire place to ourselves today.

Near the top of the old mining road, there is a turnout where I parked the Jeep head-in, so we could sit on the tailgate of the Jeep and look out over the entire expanse from a thousand feet or more above it. The views are spectacular, and the scene is always filled with all manner of wildlife. We hiked during the day and climbed into the saddle between Gold King Mountain and Dolores Peak. As evening approached, we lay in the back of the Jeep on our blankets listening to bluegrass music with a glass of wine as dusk settled in over the peaks. At one point there were elk, goats and a small family of coyotes all sharing the same basin. We cooked hamburgers and hash browns and ate chocolate chip cookies on our laps watching the sunset over the San Juan's. After sundown, we watched as the constellations unfolded above us, the north star winking at us as we laid back, drinking delicious wine and watching as sunset turned to nightfall.

"I want to tell you a story," I said.

"Go."

"After I divorced, I was alone and lonely for many years. People think that working in New York City is akin to having all kinds of dating options but actually, the opposite is true. It's incredibly hard to meet someone because everyone's in a hurry, careers come first and people's guards are always up. Anyway, I finally met a woman that I really liked – I was set up with her by a friend. I was also feeling a bit lost in my life at that point, so I tried really hard to make a solid impression – not to fabricate anything, but just to really try not to make a mistake."

"Anyway, things were going really well for maybe a month or two, and then we had our first stressful conversation, and it was shocking to me that after our conversation I could feel her taking a turn away from me. And, it wasn't even that big of a disagreement, but nonetheless it started to happen. I did everything I could to repair the situation but for whatever reason, it didn't work and she broke it off."

"Sounds like something that happens all the time to people." she said.

"Yes, but the moral of the story is that I learned that I need to share my thoughts and not hold back -- be honest and sincere and don't let any opportunity pass me by when something feels right."

"Yes, I agree," she said.

"So, I can't let this pass me by either. We've had a crazy start to our relationship because of forces outside of our control, but I want you to know I want to work hard at this. I'm all in. I don't want that to sound scary or too-early in the relationship clingy, I want it to sound loving. The reason I say this is that we only had six days in Alaska and now only three more. I need you to know how much you mean to me."

"I do," she said.

We stayed until it was entirely dark with the sky an ink black palette with bright stars littered erratically across the canvas, then unraveled from each others arms, packed up and drove the hour back to the main road.

We got back to Telluride around nine, just in time for a night cap at the New Sheridan bar before bed. We were both exhausted.

The next morning I awoke to the sound of thunder. Once again, I wasn't wearing any clothes. I raised my head to look out the window and saw that India wasn't in bed and Otter was nowhere to be seen.

I rubbed my eyes, got up, grabbed the robe from the bathroom, and walked downstairs, where I was greeted with the smell of early morning coffee and something cooking. I rounded the corner into the kitchen. India had her back to me. She was wearing her terrycloth robe and was bending over, pulling some biscuits out of the oven, talking to Otter who was watching her from the side.

"Good morning," I said.

"Good morning, sunshine."

"Why is everyone up so early would be my question. I think we should still be lounging in bed. It's stormy and that means more time in bed. Naked."

"I don't disagree. Let me finish cooking breakfast and then I'll be up to treat you to breakfast in bed. I was hoping I'd get up there before you woke up."

I hugged her from the back.

"Hurry," I said, turned, and walked back upstairs.

We decided today would be our fishing day. We had two choices – fish the San Miguel just downstream from Telluride or fish some high alpine streams that would require a hike, and would be a longer, more difficult option because access to the water would take some time. Eventually we found ourselves choosing the San Miguel, my home river. We packed a lunch, I grabbed two fly rods and a box of dry flies, and headed out. It was going to be warm today so no need for waders; we would wet wade—walk in the water with boots on but no waders.

We drove about fifteen minutes down-valley out of Telluride and turned off onto an access road west of the San Miguel County jail. I liked to start my fishing just downstream from the jail. The river was steep here, the flows were fast, and the water was extremely cold as the spot was only a couple of miles from the river's source in the canyons above Telluride. From Telluride, the San Miguel flows for 72 miles before joining the Dolores River near Uravan, and over its course falls 7,000 feet in elevation from high alpine to high desert ecosystem. The fast water around Telluride crowded the fish into obvious deep pockets and into the sharp curves of the river as it twisted its way down the steep valley. It was ideal habitat for trout. Both huge browns and rainbows lay in the deep holes and occasionally in the shallow riffles, depending on water flow, temperature, and time of year.

As we drove toward the place where we were going to fish, I told India that on the San Miguel you needed to be crafty. These fish only had four months to feed, so they were aggressive but also cagey. You typically had one shot at fooling them and the odds were stacked against you. They were sensitive to shadows and were leader-shy, and the gin-clear water gave them a perfect view of anything coming downstream. If you stood in the middle or even sometimes near the stream, you had no chance of ever catching a fish on the San Miguel. This was bank fishing, and the stealthier you were the better chance you had, plus fly placement was critical. I explained all of this in the Jeep on the way down. India was mostly silent and didn't ask questions. I sensed she had her own ideas about how this would play out. When it came to fly fishing, she was particular and she was picky. She'd spent too much time on the water to not know her way around it, and advice was only accepted if she asked for it. She looked out the window at the river as we approached; I sensed she was making judgements.

We split up. I put her on the upper portion of the river on a stretch I knew well and told her exactly what I knew about her options. I headed farther downstream to a quieter section that I knew was also good, although her section was better. Otter stayed with her. We were both fishing with light setups and large flies. It was just getting to the full-sun time of morning. We should get some action.

Once I was well downstream from her and around a bend, I set my gear against a tree and walked quietly back through the forest until I could see her. She stood still and well back from the river, just a few feet from where I had left her. She craned her neck to look over the river, examining every aspect of it, then she noticed something, took a few steps to the left, loosened her line, walked back from the water about five feet, bent forward slightly at the waist, and made a couple of false casts before dropping her fly onto a small pool on her side of the river, just off the current. The fly sat on top of the water in the quiet pool for just seconds, then it was engulfed by a huge brown, its dorsal fin piercing the surface as it headed back into the depths with its fly. She set the hook, screamed, and walked toward the water, stripping in line as she moved. Just as she reached the water she bent down and gently landed the giant brown in her hands. She was a master.

I went back, picked up my pack and entered the slower pools downstream. The water was cold but tolerable. I immediately hooked up on several large browns in the slower sections where I was fishing. It was the perfect day to fish.

After several hours of excellent action, India caught up with me and we sat on a huge flat boulder that stuck out into the river. The boulder was about ten feet wide and four feet high, high enough that we were well off the water. The river was wider and slower here than where we started and about thirty feet across. There was dense forest behind us and there were red canyon walls on the other side of the river facing us; the canyon walls shot straight up 100 feet or more at the water's edge, curving and concave in appearance. It was late morning and we were getting a full sun hit. We felt lazy, and eventually we lay back on the rock, putting our small backpacks beneath our heads. Otter lay beside us on the fleece jacket I had taken off as the morning got warmer. The sky was sapphire blue without a single blemish and the wind was calm.

"You know what I think?" India said.

"I'd give anything to know."

"You should move here."

"Yeah. I know. Everyone says that. I've toyed with it for years. If I didn't have that work thing, I would. But honestly, I get a bit lonely here. I only know a few people and I only have one person I would call a friend. It's just Otter and me 95 percent of the time and that can get isolating and lonely, no matter how busy you make yourself or how much you ski or fish or hike. But even with that said, I think I'll end up here eventually. It's just a matter of when and what it will look like." I paused and chose my next words carefully as we made eye contact.

"Here's the deal. And I'm serious. I'll move here if you'll move here."

"Humm. That requires some consideration. Before I get to that, and the reason

I say you should move here - it's just that your house is amazing. I absolutely love everything about it. It's stunning and the perfect place to live in what appears to be the perfect mountain town. I can't imagine what it's like here in the winter. It must be just as magical with the views and these mountains."

"That's a whole other story. We average around 175 inches of snow a year in town. That's 14 feet."

"Do you have a caretaker or someone who deals with your house then? Do you come out in the winter?"

"Yes, I have a caretaker, and yes, I come here and ski, and the skiing is fantastic. But honestly, from Thanksgiving through early April, the snow is unrelenting. As much as I love to ski and enjoy the snow, I frankly prefer the summer months because of the range of activities. You literally can't do much of anything but ski in the winter. It's intense, but then I guess you know a thing or two about that from Alaska.

"But, getting back to your original point, I do think about moving here all the time, but there needs to be more for me here than just me. I need to start thinking about putting together a meaningful relationship with someone who sees the things in Telluride that I see. Who wants to participate in both the winter and summer seasons here and not get bored or overwhelmed or whatever. I'm getting to a point where it's not healthy to be on my own for this long. I need to make that change in my life. My problem is that I'm never alone but I'm always lonely. I can't seem to complete the loop."

"But it's not like you can click your heals and find the woman of your dreams and boom, you're here and everything's perfect. That's going to take time and a lot of doing to accomplish. What are you going to do in the meantime, continue to wander between New York and the Adirondacks and Telluride? That sounds like a lot of wandering without a solid plan. Or maybe not, that's just how it strikes me."

"That's true. I need to find some clarity in my life real soon. I've been out on a line, walking a tightrope, for many years now, and I need to stop the wandering." I paused and swallowed hard. "So, point well stated. Maybe you can help. I'm not that bad of a catch."

"No, you're absolutely not," she said, laughing. "You're anything but a bad catch."

"Then let's stay in Telluride together and see what the future holds. I'm serious. If you move here so will I."

"Okay, you're giving me a lot to think about Eli and I will. In the meantime, let's have lunch."

She looked over at me and smiled. We got quiet after that. After a few minutes she sat up and started undoing our backpack, pulling out the water bottles, then taking out the wine, and finally pulling out our lunch. I started up the camp stove and made us macaroni and cheese with river water while she made chicken salad sandwiches using the last of our bakery bread. We sat in silence, watching a family of river otters playing on the far side of the river. I waited for India to respond to my proposal, to tell me she would come here and live with me or say no, but she said nothing, and the longer I waited the more unsettled I became.

We spent the balance of the day continuing our fishing, lazily casting our lines in promising pools. We caught fish all day. The rainbows and browns were plentiful and hungry and our dry flies were on fire.

Eventually we walked the three miles back to the Jeep and drove back to the house. We napped on the deck until the long rays of the afternoon sun began to wane and early evening settled in. It was cool in the shadows of the deck and we both wrapped blankets around us. Tonight, I was taking her to the Embers Restaurant in the Western Hotel. My favorite place in town. We were both starving.

I sat on the old period sofa with Queen Anne legs and a faded green tapestry print in the living room with Otter beside me, waiting for India to come down after her bath. I had made a small fire in the fireplace, which was my favorite part of the house. The mantle was 4 feet high with a 3 feet top that was a beveled German mirror. The facing had blue embossed 6-inch tiles and the hearth itself was massive – 5 feet by 20 inches with enameled tiles and an embossed tile border. It was spectacular and spread its warmth like luxurious tentacles throughout the room.

India was luxuriating in the bath, and once again I could hear her softly singing a song that I couldn't place. She'd lit candles in the bathroom when she was filling the white porcelain clawfoot tub with steaming hot water and bath salts, and she'd asked me to open the window to let in the chilled early evening air, making even more than the normal amount of thick steam roll off the bath water. I turned off some of the overhead lights. When she stepped into the tub, she sighed with contentment and I knew it would be some time before she was out. She lay back, her long hair hanging over the edge and spreading out over the floor. I got the sense she hadn't relaxed in a bath that nice in some time. I had half a mind to join her when she asked me, but

I decided to let her have the full benefit of the tub to herself.

The moon was full and bright and moonbeams cast erratic shadows around the darkened living room where I sat now, waiting in the lamplight. I had on one small, old, Capodimonte lamp with a hoop shade with fringe, that sat in the corner. The lamp came with the house and I suspected it must date back at least to the early 1900's. I rarely sat in here but tonight it seemed right. I was streaming a quiet mix of western music through the house as we got ready. It felt good to sit and relax as the music bounced around the high-ceilinged rooms, echoing off the tin ceilings and plaster walls. I had a large glass of wine and looked over a copy of the Telluride Daily Planet which had been thrown onto the front steps while we were gone earlier in the day.

After an hour or so I heard India's footsteps on the stairs. She came down the curved walnut staircase dressed in a short dark-navy dress, her hair down around her waist, sandals replacing her sneakers and a gold locket around her neck. I had never seen her look this dressed up. She was the most beautiful woman I had ever seen.

I set my wine glass down, walked over to her, put my arms around her waist, and gently kissed her. Her clean scent enveloped me and for a moment I forgot my anxiety about whether she was going to respond to my invitation to move in with me here.

"You look beautiful. I'm the luckiest man in the world tonight."

"Thank you."

The next day we went to Ptarmigan Lake, which sits at just over 13,000 feet in elevation. It's just off the Jeep trail that runs from Telluride to Ouray. As the Jeep trail crosses Imogene Pass, locals know there is a trail leading to the lake just behind a small hill after the summit. If you weren't aware the lake was there, you wouldn't have any idea it was just over the rise. It's a glacial lake that sits in a bowl behind the Pass. The lake usually has snow on it year round, and often ice never completely leaves the water's surface. I had found the lake by looking carefully at a backcountry map and then bushwhacked there many years before.

Only a few blocks from my house is Tomboy Road, which leads to Imogene Pass. Tomboy Road first leads to the abandoned mining town of Tomboy, a town from the 1880's that used to have 1,000-year round residents. Once you pass Tomboy, you continue up the pass road and at 13,114 feet, you reach the pass. I parked my Jeep just off the road at the top and accessed the lake from there.

On the south side of the lake is a small shack that is in surprisingly good condition given the altitude and it's age, which must date back to at least the late 1880's, around the time the town of Tomboy was still inexistence. I have always presumed that the severity of the cold must have preserved the shack remnants over the past hundred years or so but I'm not sure. I'm also unsure if the shack was built by workers who ran electricity over the pass or someone else, but I couldn't imagine who. It was a two-room shack that had a small living area with old wood stove and then a bedroom with bunk beds that were still in place. The floor was rotted out but the tin roof still kept most of the elements out and a few windows were still in place.

We got to the lake area at about one. The day had cleared off nicely and we were down to shorts and long-sleeved shirts by the time we left the Jeep and started walking the mile to the lake. We were going to have a late lunch in the shack, or lake side, which was now a more likely option given the beautiful weather.

We got to the lake and decided to eat our lunch on a flat boulder beside the water. We had sandwiches and some soup we had picked up from Smith's Market, just like the day before. I'd brought a camp stove to heat up the soup. After lunch we lay back on the boulder and took a sun bath while Otter explored the shore and chased the Marmot and Pika that were taunting her from their rock lairs.

India reached over her hand while we lay beside each other on the rock. "Thank you for arranging all of this and for inviting me," she said. "It's a magical place and I'm so glad I came. I'm lucky to be able to experience this with you."

"My pleasure. We didn't have enough time before and not enough time here either. I missed you badly after I left Alaska." It had been a month since we were together in Alaska. I glanced at her. She was looking at me intently. This was it, I thought.

Just then we heard a small rockslide behind us. We looked over and saw a herd of mountain goats standing on a ledge above us staring at Otter, who was frozen in place. The goats spotted us, and after a few minutes they turned and walked off to the mountain they had presumable come in from. We turned back to each other.

India took a deep breath. "So, what now?" she asked.

"I was about to ask you the same thing."

"I'm leaving in two weeks to go surfing in Mexico for the winter. My sister and I make a trip every year. Sometimes it's Mexico and sometimes it's Hawaii – this year it's Mexico."

"I recall you mentioning that. Any chance you could come to New York before you go? Or could I meet you somewhere along the route in California?"

"I don't know. I'll have to think and talk to my sister. We've had these plans for months and it's just not my schedule but hers as well. If it was just me, I would see you again soon. I want you to know that. I would see you again very soon."

"India, there's something I want you to know. I need to say it to you or I'll never be able to come to terms with what happened between us in Alaska and now here. I'll never be able square this in my mind, in my life, if I don't talk this out."

"Okay."

"In spite of what you may see as my self-confidence or my success, I'm really uncertain about where I'm going in life. I wake up in the middle of the night I worry about my heart. I worry about never finding someone who can inspire me the way I inspire her. I worry about finding love. I worry about finding you. And now that I've found you I don't want to let you go."

"I know, Eli. I get it and I feel strongly about you too. I also don't want to let this go. But for me it's not so easy. It's not so definite."

"Why?"

"Because I'm a bit of a loner. I've never had a seriously committed relationship and I tend to take things slower than you, I think. Our time together in Alaska and here has had a huge impact on me. I'm having new feelings that I've never had before, and I just need some time to think things over. That isn't a bad thing or a bad response. It's actually the opposite. I've been so moved by our time together that I'm seeing options for my life that I haven't had before. So take this the right way. I've never met anyone like you and I'm excited, but I need to think. And I need to keep my promise to my sister and head to Mexico. I'll think about how I can work you into that."

"Okay," I said. "Do you promise?"

"Of course, I promise."

The Telluride summer music scene is bookended by the Telluride Bluegrass Festival, which is held in mid-June, and the Blues and Brews Festival, which is in September. As a matter of routine every year, I purchased passes to both festivals and kept them at the house. Tonight, our last night in Telluride, was the final show of the Blues and Brews Festival. Joe Cocker was playing, and we planned to attend.

We got back to the house from Ptarmigan lake around four thirty and took a nap on the deck under the giant pine and the now just-changing-to-fall Aspens. Their deep green leaves just showing signs of yellow and quaking in the breeze as they began to dry out and transition to full yellow before falling. After our naps, I suggested we go to City Park where the concert was and hit a few of the beer tents and have a casual dinner, after which we would catch the show.

It was getting cooler. We put on long pants, long-sleeved shirts and hoodies to ward off the chilly night air that would descend on us once the sun went down. City Park sits toward the back of the box canyon that Telluride sits in and is ringed by the high peaks surrounding Telluride. When the sun is out, it is bathed in full-hit sunshine but when the sun drops behind the peaks, the park is plunged into near darkness and it's chilly even in mid-summer. We hopped on the two bikes that I kept at the house and pedaled our way to City Park and spent the balance of the late afternoon and early evening walking among food and craft vendors who lined the outside ring of the outdoor music venue. We held hands and laughed as we walked and drank beers and had dinner on plates held on our laps, looking up at Bridal Veil Falls towering a thousand feet above us as the warm-up band's music filled the air.

Joe Cocker was as good as advertised. We finished dinner, went into the venue and danced in each other's arms, drank too much beer and before we knew it, the concert and our night was over. It was nearing midnight by the time we pedaled back to the house, singing the lyrics from *I Get By With A Little Help From My Friends* the entire way home.

Her flight was at ten the next morning and we had to leave the house by six-thirty.

"How about one more nightcap on the deck." I said.

"Of course, but I think that's sad."

"Me too."

I set two alarms just in case we had a power issue or God forbid, we simply overslept. They both went off at five-forty-five and after I turned them off and made sure she was awake, I went downstairs to start the coffee. As I was leaving the bedroom I looked back and she had already begun packing her backpack in the still darkness of the cool early morning.

A few minutes later she came down into the kitchen and I handed her a travel mug of coffee.

"Here's your wake-up coffee for the road. I'm going to let Otter out and warm-up the Jeep – be right back."

"Okay."

I let Otter out while I started the Jeep and put India's larger backpack in the back. We were ready to go. I looked up at the house from the drive. The lights cast a tinted yellow glow in the early morning hours. The house looked lived in like it had felt for the past few days. I didn't want this memory to end.

We walked out the front door with Otter and climbed into the Jeep. It was a chilly early morning but beautiful as the sky to the east began to be illuminated by a striking orange glow that had yet to crest the mountains behind the house. The orange glow contrasted with the deep dark, nearly black sky to the west that hadn't yet started the transition to sunrise. As we backed out of the drive, I turned up the heat in the Jeep and we started our drive out of Telluride. We were the only car on the road.

"Wait," India said. I braked and looked over at her.

"Can we please take one more drive through town before we leave? I want to see everything once more before I leave."

"Of course."

I turned left on Colorado Avenue and drove slowly by the now-closed shops and restaurants we had visited over the past few days. India stared out the windows as we passed Fir, Pine, Spruce, and Willow streets and headed down toward the park where we had been last night. I made a wide U-turn on Columbine Street at the end of town, then proceeded back the way we had come, passing the Western Hotel, the Embers Restaurant and finally returning to the spot at the corner of Aspen and Colorado where we had started. I stopped the car just outside the courthouse and looked over at India. She stared straight ahead and I could see she had tears in her eyes, as did I. I put the car back in gear and drove out of town.

Driving down off the Uncompahgre Plateau out of Telluride is a sight to behold with the soaring San Juan's fading gradually into the high ranges of the Plateau, and in this early morning, the sky was a watercolor menagerie of golds, oranges, blues and watermelon reds unlike anything I had ever seen before. About 30 minutes into the silent and somber drive, India had finished her coffee and lay down across the front bench seat, put her head in my lap and fell fast asleep. I covered her with my coat. I looked in the back and Otter was also asleep. I had the car to myself and I stroked India's hair as she slept and tried to memorize every perfect and imperfect feature of her face.

At the airport I carried her backpack to the check-in counter. She checked her bag and we walked to the same restaurant I had gotten my coffee in when she arrived four days ago. We sat for a few moments, both of us visibly shaken.

"I don't know what to say. I'm not good at goodbyes" I said. "And in this moment I'm at a loss for words. I'm incredibly sad."

"I'm sad too," she said. I'll never forget this weekend or forget you. I think we should just leave it at that. I'll call you when I get home to let you know I made it and we can talk more then. Now's not a good time for either of us. Is that okay?"

"No but yes."

At the security area she put her things on the belt, then turned to me and we hugged. I kissed her and she proceeded through security without looking back.

I pulled over to a parking area that overlooked the runway and sat there in the Jeep. After forty minutes or so, I saw her plane taxi out to the end of the runway, turn and accelerate down the runway, then fly off into the pale blue sky of an otherwise perfect Colorado morning.

EPILOGUE

"If I had a flower for every time, I think of you,
I could walk through my garden forever."

—Alfred Tennyson

The subway doors slammed shut and the 5-train lurched into motion with a screech. A garbled announcement came over the speaker from the faceless, nameless conductor tucked away in a secret compartment somewhere out of sight. The early morning New York City subway train was packed with businesspeople huddled with their papers and their phones and their jackets, with construction workers heading to their jobs with their hard hats tethered to their waists, many of them asleep in their seat. Teachers, children, and families sitting together with the random homeless person here and there. The train hurled south along the Lexington Avenue line toward lower Manhattan from Grand Central, where I had gotten on. At each stop; 14th Street, Brooklyn Bridge/City Hall, Fulton Street and finally Wall Street, I was shocked back to reality every time the train screeched to a stop. The doors opened and closed, rudely discharging and reloading the legion of impersonal commuters making their way through New York's underground maze today like every other day. A careless and uncontrolled mass bumping and grinding as they made their way to their destinations, all the while careful to not make eye contact.

The contrast was shocking. The noise and confusion and chaos of this existence compared to the beauty and simplicity of where I had been over the past few weeks was a total shock to my system and my life.

More importantly, I was shocked by the loss of India, the loss of hope and potential, the loss of love. I was back in New York from my whirlwind trips to Alaska and Telluride. Yet at the same time, maybe I wasn't. Maybe I was back in Alaska or maybe in Telluride. Maybe I was in a wide valley ringed with snowcapped mountains or maybe creaking my way through my old Victorian house on West Columbia Avenue on a Sunday morning with Otter and a cup of coffee. Or maybe I was casting a lonely line to a fish who couldn't know half my troubles.

"I've looked at love from both sides now, from give and take and still somehow It's love's illusions I recall, I really don't know love at all."

—Joni Mitchell

JEFFREY GRISAMORE is a New York City based agency executive who spends his free time writing and in pursuit of a wide range of outdoor activities, including climbing, biking, motorcycling and most of all, fishing. His travels for business and pleasure have taken him around the world, almost always with a fly rod in tow. *Six Days in September* is his first novel and his second, *Valentine*, is scheduled for release in early 2022. Jeffrey divides his time between New York City, his native Iowa, and Salida, Colorado.